LEGACY *of* LIGHTNING

RISE OF THE HOTARU ONNA-MUSHA

JOHN EUDY

ISBN 978-1-68570-760-6 (paperback)
ISBN 978-1-68570-761-3 (digital)

Christian Faith Publishing
832 Park Avenue
Meadville, PA 16335
www.christianfaithpublishing.com

Printed in the United States of America

For our daughters…

CONTENTS

CHAPTER 1

Kumo and the Jilted Suitor

Takeda Kenshin is the Hotaru-Raikō's daimyō. He and his kind are unique to this world: human in form but endowed with slender antennae, smoke-colored wings, and thin, yet sturdy, coal-black wing covers of a firefly. Although their eyes are dark ebony, they are almond shaped instead of round, like their firefly cousins. Their skin is fair and pale, while their fine hair is long and black like their antennae. Women wear their hair long and straight, letting their antennae flow backward with their hair, while the men often arrange their topknot so it rests between their antennae.

Long ago, the Hotaru-Raikō, as they are known now, once danced above the lush, grassy fields around the great tree of life. Unfortunately, they committed an act of selfish pride, which offended Kami, the one true God. However, unlike Akuma, the traitor, who was cast down from Tengoku,[1] the hotaru were shown mercy. Though disgraced, they were sent out of the great garden to live in the land of Nihon. For hundreds of years, Takeda-san and his clan lived on the outskirts of human civilization, peacefully sharing the lands with man,

---

[1] Heaven (translated from Japanese).

who saw them as beautiful and benevolent creatures. Always watching and studying, the hotaru learned much, even adopting some of man's customs and culture. In time, man began to develop the land and use natural resources for his own purposes. This created a divide between the two races and a wariness of the hotaru clan. They began to move, building their own temporary settlements near the villages of men, but not close enough to be seen. If they happened to be discovered, the clan would move to the borders of another village.

It was at the beginning of what came to be known as the Heian period that Takeda-san and his clan finally settled in the Echizen Province. There, on the sunnier, south side of the Fukui Castle moat, among a dense thicket, lies an old, long-forgotten ishidōrō.[2] A verdant moss adorns its hand-chiseled roof, while mint-colored lichen blankets the pitted gray stone upon which the lantern rests. It likely illuminated a road or a path to an ancient shrine once, but the hotaru quickly dedicated it to God and made it the center of their village. Now there is a well-worn path leading up to its simple openings where the flame of man once dwelt. Long bladed grasses gently reach up on either side of the ascendant trail like curved, oceanic waves crashing on a rocky shore. Though they could easily fly up to the shrine entrance, the hotaru prefer to approach humbly on foot between the swaying grasses.

To the north of Fukui Castle where man dwells, there a military governor holds court in the fortified residence. He acts as landlord for local farmers, and his retainers provide protection for them. Between them and the Raikō clan is a large moat, the waters of which gently lap the sandy shore leading up to the woodland undergrowth. Inside the thicket, the clan has built an earthen wall to surround their daimyō's austere, shinden-style estate. The shinden (main hall) itself

---

2   Stone lantern (translated from Japanese).

sits directly north of the shrine. Covered breezeways stretch out to tainoya (additional or guest houses) on both the eastern and western sides of the main hall. Small tea trees grow in each of the rectangular enclosures between the tainoya and shinden. Leading south out of each tainoya toward the shrine are two enclosed walkways called rō. As is customary, inner gates were built in the middle of each rō, both of which line up with the east and west outer gates in the earthen wall. On the southern end of the western rō is an enclosed pavilion with a view of the niwa, or courtyard garden, and the torii leading up to the shrine. On the eastern side is a rectangular open-air pavilion, which is the best place to view both the moonrise and Mount Haku, or Hakusan, in the east. The uncomplicated aesthetics of Heian architecture lend to the natural beauty of the shinden estate.

The niwa between the shinden and the shrine is wide open. It is here, beneath the towering shrine, the clan occasionally gathers for theater, kyūdō[3] contests, and Takeda-san's favorite sport, Sumai no Sechi, which was a precursor to sumo wrestling. The object of the Raikō version of Sumai no Sechi is to grapple one's opponent to the ground, forcing them to their back inside a ring on the ground made of heavy rope. The real challenge is that neither opponent can open their wing covers; they are prohibited from flying. The daimyō, his samurai, and several of his trusted warriors watch intently, making wagers on the matches and getting slightly boisterous depending on the outcome. Conversely, whenever the warriors are away, Harumi, Takeda-san's beloved wife, allows the children to play kemari[4] in the courtyard. She prefers their laughter and merriment to wrestling.

Just past the shrine, the earthen wall surrounding the estate gives way to walls of woven willow branches, which protect the rest of the village. The rest of the clan has built their family homes in this area south of the shrine. Some built simple wooden homes with flared, thatched rooves, somewhat reminiscent of the older, Yayoi architecture. Some elevated their homes on posts, while others combined stone and wood to build into the surrounding thicket. Entering through the southern gate, one would get a sense of a rustic, tranquil, and inviting village at one with the natural environment, as though it had been there for ages.

To the north, on the outer banks of the castle moat, where the water is shallow, the lotus lilies grow large and luxuriant. Once the cherry blossoms have run their course, Harumi can sometimes be found seen sitting on a tall blade of grass rising out of the eastern corner of the earthen wall.

---

[3] Archery (translated from Japanese).
[4] A game that resembles a combination of soccer and hacky sack.

From that most excellent vantage point, she contemplatively stares out across the lotus fields. She is captivated by the gentle and vibrant flowers dotting the field of giant green pads floating in the clear and gleaming water. Each flower makes a subtle transition from a vivid, pink tip down to a pure, soft white bottom on their petals. Bright-yellow stigmas resting at the center of each flower, like the sun, invite the dragonfly and the bee to visit. She always finds peace watching life unfold on the moat.

It was in this idyllic setting that many of the hotaru warriors became especially intrigued with the burgeoning philosophy of Bushido, the way of the warrior. Historically, the men of Nihon were fascinated by war and military valor. Though they lacked true knowledge of Kami, the one true God, the people of the island nation cherished the beauty of nature, reason, and self-discipline. Additionally, though warlike in their nature, the people practiced a strict moral code; unnecessary killing, thievery, intoxication, sexual misconduct, and bearing false witness were strictly forbidden. Takeda-san and his people quickly see the benefits of Bushido in their pursuit of a disciplined and moral earthly life. They look for avenues to fully integrate the way of the samurai into their culture. It was in this pursuit that they came to pledge their lives to the protection of their weaker cousins, the Hotaru no Chikyū.[5] It was Hotaru-himē, the daughter of Hi-ō, lord of the Hotaru no Chikyū, who gave them the Hotaru-Raikō name. She said the white light of their armor and weapons reminded her of the lightning that spans earth and sky.

As a matter of circumstance, it was after the wedding of Hotaru-himē[6] to her prince, Hi-marō, that Takeda-san became acutely aware of the fact he has only one child, a

---

[5] Firefly of the earth (translated from Japanese).
[6] See *Guardian of the Lightning Seeds* for the full legend.

daughter, and that he has no male heir to take his place as daimyō. He is not alone in this observation either. A young warrior named Ishida sees this too. Ishida is a cunning warrior, not much older than the daimyō's daughter. Like her, he was born in this world long after the Hotaru-Raikō were sent out of the garden. Ishida sometimes displays a greater love for this world than he does for their true home. He harbors an unspoken envy of Takeda-san deep within his materialistic heart. He craves worldly title and power. He wants to live in the palace, control the shrine, and lord over the clan. He knows if he can win the hand of the daimyō's daughter and marry her, he will become the heir apparent, eventually replacing Takeda. So, unbeknownst to anyone, Ishida makes plans to secretly court the seventeen-year-old Ashi.

Ashi is a clever young woman, highly observant of her surroundings. Within her kind and generous heart, she carries a quiet passion for Kami, a pure and innocent love of God. Because of this love, she has the gift of being able to sense other's auras. Unlike man, who primarily sees only physical expressions, the elder hotaru, as well as Ashi, can see the internal light, or darkness, of others. Outwardly, like her father, she is also incredibly observant of her surroundings. On one brisk, autumn morning at the village market, her talent will change the fortunes of many of her clansmen.

It is early, and there are few others around. Ashi browses the market for berries and mushrooms. She is alone. Ishida discovers her there. He stalks her as she peruses the grocer's baskets. His light is dim, and he wears the brim of his bamboo sandogasa[7] down over his eyes so as to not attract any undue attention from others. He draws close to her and, standing just behind and to her right, offers a soft greeting, "Good morning, Ashi-san." Ashi glances in Ishida's direction,

---

[7] Conical-style hat (translated from Japanese).

recognizing him immediately. He smiles coyly when she does and says, "Utsukushii.[8] You really are beautiful." Normally Ashi would just keep her head slightly downward when one of the samurai spoke, but he is not samurai yet. His words have also made her feel uncomfortable. The presumptuous compliment prompts her to turn and tilt her head slightly. He lifts his head, too, so she can see into his eyes.

She peers at him out of the sides of her own eyes, staring deeply into the windows of his soul. There is something dark and selfish in him. She sees lust and greed lurking in his shadowy light. She mutters in reaction to what she sees, "Īe!"[9] Ishida instantly feels the sting of her sudden and flat rejection. He gasps before taking a half step back from her in shock.

Ashi realizes what she has done. She never meant to say it out loud, but she has deeply offended Ishida with that one word. Wanting to escape the situation, she quickly collects her items and then hurriedly leaves the market. Ishida looks around anxiously, feeling as though everyone in the village saw her rejection of him. Though it went unseen by all, a sense of shame still fills him. It is a feeling he does not like, and it quickly leads to anger.

He looks up the road where Ashi rushes to return home. She has accidentally dropped one of her items on the road. Another young warrior in training, Saitō Sōji, stops to pick up the package and politely hand it back to her. Although Ishida cannot hear what is said, it is obvious Ashi is grateful for Saitō's assistance. She hurriedly bows before rushing toward the estate while he moves on as though he had done nothing. Jealousy and resentment swell in Ishida's heart and mind. He slips behind the market to angrily pace in the alley

---

[8] Beautiful (translated from Japanese).

[9] Pronounced "Ee-yay"—meaning "No" (translated from Japanese).

near the wall of willow branches. He is uncertain how the daimyō will react to his advances toward Ashi. Fear and anger lead him to take flight and leave the village.

He flies through the forest in short bursts, moving from branch to branch, landing only long enough to brood on his malcontent. Because of their size, the Hotaru-Raikō have few enemies and are usually free to move about the fields and forests unmolested. Not even man has trails in this area of the woods. So he continues to fly about the red, orange, and yellow autumn foliage, consumed by his own selfish thoughts. As he flies, he is not aware of the changes around him. The normally bright, autumn beauty of the woods gives way to a darker, more shadowy sky than usual. The air grows stale, quiet, ominous, but he does not notice because of his self-absorbed brooding. Ishida does not see the massive web, set between two old, leafless trees, swaying back and forth in the stale air. He flies headlong into it and is immediately trapped by the sticky silk.

Because the hotaru fly with their bodies upright, unlike birds that fly horizontally, nearly his entire body is stuck. Only his wing shells remain free. Ishida stays still for a few seconds, looking around cautiously. He has been trapped somewhere near the bottom half of the massive web. There are many husks on the ground below, some the size of small birds. The air smells of death and decay. Even the slight breeze that sways the web cannot carry the stench away. Nothing is moving; there is no sound. Feeling only a little confident that it is an old, unoccupied web, he tries to reach for the tantō in his obi.[10] Unfortunately, he cannot reach it or either of his swords. He yanks his right arm, trying to break the web so he can reach them, but to no avail. He rests for a moment on the web, which bounces like a trampoline. Then he hears it.

---

[10] Belt (translated from Japanese).

One of the radial lines of the web is plucked like the string on a biwa,[11] reverberating down to where he is.

Ishida remains as still as he can. There comes another pluck of the line, harder this time, making the capture web ripple. He can feel an evil presence; he knows he is not alone. An uneasiness arises in his stomach. He knows he cannot escape but also knows he must reach his tantō or wakizashi[12] if he is to survive. He struggles to free his right arm, shaking the web. He hears movement above and suddenly stops. He looks up to see a massive, dark body. Several red eyes peer down upon him. Panic begins to set in. If he does not free his hand, he will die a gruesome and dishonorable death. He looks back down to see how close his hand is to his tantō. The spider violently bounces the whole web, causing him to become even more entangled. Thoroughly ensnared, he knows he is about to meet his end. He turns his eyes toward the shadowy figure above and finds that it has changed.

There are now only two red eyes looking down at him. The spider creature turns its body, and Ishida can no longer see its eyes. He can, however, just make out the spindly, hairy black legs starting to move down the webbing. It casts a web into the tree canopy and swings out away from the web. Descending slowly on the silken thread, a human figure begins to come into the light. He is surprised to see the delicate feet of a woman appear first. Then the rest of her is slowly revealed in the light. The woman is as big as he is. She has fair skin and long, ebony hair, which is somewhat disheveled. She wears a three-layer jūnihitoe.[13] The inner robe is a white kosode, which is covered by a crimson hitoe robe.

---

[11] Japanese lute, a stringed instrument (translated from Japanese).
[12] Smaller sword, similar to the modern katana.
[13] Layered robes, a precursor to the modern kimono (translated from Japanese).

And then there's a final black uchigi, or outer robe. It is all loosely tied together with a golden obi, which allows more of her milky skin above her bosom to be visible. The skinny, black legs protrude from her back and hold onto the strand from which she has descended. Ishida finds himself strangely mesmerized by this yōkai.[14]

Curiously, the spider yōkai does not race down the web to inject her venom. Instead, she moves slowly, seductively, toward Ishida. She immediately recognizes the crest on his kataginu[15]; she knows from where he comes. She reaches out with her hands to grasp the webbing around him, slightly pressing herself against him. "Well," she whispers, "who has come to visit me today?" Ishida's eyes are transfixed on her round crimson eyes; he does not notice her gently breaking the webbing around his wings. He does feel when they are loosened though and instinctively lowers them. "Mmmm," moans Kumo, while she guides his wings under their ebony shells. "How delicate and strong," she whispers in his ear, all while secretly ensuring the excess webbing has locked his wings closed, preventing his flight. She then moves swiftly to his left side; he turns his head to find her. She slips her hand just inside the edge of his kosode and slowly slides it down to his obi. Again, she groans, "Ohhh." Ishida is becoming aroused by her. She grasps the sheaths of his blades, gently removing them from his obi. "You weren't going to use these on me, were you?" she asks innocently.

"Ie," he answers humbly.

"Yoi,"[16] she says with a seductive smile. She lifts the swords and tantō in the air over her head, and one of her

---

[14] Supernatural creatures or spirits often considered demons (translated from Japanese).
[15] Short sleeveless garment (translated from Japanese).
[16] Pronounced "Yoh-ee"—meaning "Good" (translated from Japanese).

spindly legs takes them and secures them to the strand of web she descended on. Now that his weapons are out of reach, she begins to slowly cut the strands of webbing from around Ishida. "I am Kumo." She pauses. "I have been waiting for you, samurai, waiting for a long time." She stops and looks deeply into his eyes; she is expecting him to introduce himself.

"Ishida," he mumbles.

"Ah," she acknowledges as she returns to cutting the webbing. "I have need of a fearless samurai...Ishida." Finished clipping the webbing on his left side, she rolls him over on his back on the web. He is now completely helpless before her. Kumo lets go of the ensnaring web. She now dangles gracefully just in front of him. Her jūnihitoe nearly slips off her left shoulder as she sways on the strand. Ishida ogles her as she pulls it back up. She sees the lust in his eyes. "Where do your loyalties lie, young Ishida? Who is your master?"

"I am rōnin, my lady."

"Are you not of the Hotaru-Raikō clan?"

"No longer. I would have my own clan," boasts Ishida.

Kumo senses this is her opportunity. "Yoi," she says with a grin as she boldly touches his chest. "Are there others you hold sway over, young warrior?"

"Hai.[17] A handful."

Kumo pulls herself close to Ishida, her own robes again touching his. "I have a proposition for you, samurai." Her tiny white fangs glint in the light as she smiles at him. "Your old daimyō stands in the way of what I intend to accomplish. If you help me, I will install you as lord in his place." She puts her lips close to his ear. "If you bring those loyal to you, to serve me, I will not only give you back your blades but

---

[17] Yes (translated from Japanese).

everything else your heart desires. Will you do this for me...
koibito?"[18] A lustful shiver moves through Ishida.
"Hai," answers Ishida obediently. In that moment, he
is fully given over to lust and greed. An unholy bargain is
struck. Kumo snips the last strands of webbing and those
holding his wings to his body. Ishida flies out in front of the
web and turns to bow to his new master.

"You will find me in the forest between the Kutsuki
Valley and the Saba Kaido in the Kyoto Province. Seek out
my webbed palace in the beech tree at the center of the
woods."

"Hai," he agrees. Ishida bows again and then flies back
into the forest from which he came.

Kumo continues to grin with a wicked pleasure.

*****

It was no coincidence that Saitō was near the market
that morning. He, too, is enamored of Ashi and was hoping simply to get a glimpse of her gliding through the village. Saitō is only a year older than Ashi. He is handsome
and strong, yet humble, studious, and hardworking. Every
morning he rises, cares for his hygiene, goes to the shrine in
reverence of God, prays for the souls of his parents, and then
eats. He practices his swordsmanship and archery daily. His
goal is to fly with the daimyō one day as one of his trusted
samurai. Unlike Ishida however, Saitō does not see Ashi as
a means to an end, rather he sees the inner beauty of her
heart, which radiates outward. He knows her way, her movements, her smile, her strength, her voice, and her light; he is
attracted to everything about her. Though he does not have
much to offer in the way of gifts, nothing that might win her

---

[18] Lover (translated from Japanese).

hand anyway, he hopes she might notice his own light, which burns brightly for her.

Although he was all too eager to help, he made a concerted effort to keep propriety in mind while in the public square as he helped her with the package she dropped when fleeing the market that morning. The last thing he wanted was to bring any shame upon her. Her kind words and smile made it difficult for Saitō to walk away that morning. Speaking to her made his heart thunder against his chest, he struggled to keep calm. After that brief encounter, he boldly resolved to request an audience with her father later that day. He was even more thrilled when he received word the same evening that his request was granted. He was to meet with Ashi's father the next morning.

*****

It is a chilly morning. Takeda-san finds Saitō waiting patiently at the eastern inner gate. He approaches him, and Saitō offers a deep bow. "Good morning, masutā."[19]

"Good morning, Saitō-san." Takeda-san returns a slight bow. Afterward, he waves his hand, inviting him into the courtyard. "Kuru.[20] Walk with me." He turns to stroll across the niwa. Saitō follows to his left. "I hear good things about you. Hatano-san informs me you are becoming a skilled and proficient warrior. I also understand you assisted my daughter yesterday in the market. Seems your assistance, and your respect for her, has caught her eye. Now, here you are…wishing to speak with me."

"Hai." Saitō swallows his throbbing heart back down into his chest and summons his courage. "It is true I wish to

---

[19] Master (translated from Japanese).
[20] Come (translated from Japanese).

19

serve as one of your ashigaru,[21] but more than that…" There is a brief silence. Only the crunching of gravel can be heard underfoot. "Though I know it is bold of me, I would ask your permission to court Ashi."

Takeda stops in his tracks. He turns to look into Saitō's eyes, who has also stopped and stands upright before him. Takeda sees both humility and courage in the young warrior. "Why do you seek my daughter's hand?" he asks in a firm, deep voice. He tests the motives of the young hotaru.

"Truly, it is the light of her heart that attracts me. Her outer beauty is reflective of her mind, her heart, and her grace. All I ask is the opportunity to win her favor. Nothing more."

"And if she rejects your advances?"

"I am still your loyal servant, masutā. My sword and my life are yours to command." He offers a humble bow.

"Hrmm," grumbles Takeda as he turns and quietly continues his stroll. Saitō raises back up and follows. They walk in silence toward the western gate. A large autumn leaf gently lands on the ground near them, but neither pays it much attention. They stop near the gate. Takeda turns to face the young warrior. "Your request is granted, Saitō-san. I am pleased with your courage and your courtesy. I will allow you to speak with Ashi. I will tell her you will seek her out soon."

"Dōmo arigatōgozaimashita!"[22] Saitō responds, restraining his elation as he bows. Takeda-san bows slightly in return. Although Saitō exits the niwa calmly, he is barely able to contain his jubilation as he returns swiftly toward his humble home.

---

[21] Foot soldiers (translated from Japanese).
[22] Thank you very much (translated from Japanese).

Takeda takes a deep breath of crisp fall air and then turns back toward the shinden. *Is my shōjo*[23] *really of age? So much time has passed,* he thinks.

*****

Ishida returns to Raikō Village two days after the incident in the market. He delayed his return, taking the time to plot his next move. He arrives quietly in the morning when most of the village still sleeps. Visiting a fellow warrior, he learns of Ashi's courtship with Saitō; the whole village is abuzz with excitement over it. Ishida asks his host to discretely call the rest of their closest friends to a meet under the large cherry tree east of the village in an hour. He stresses they are to tell no one. "While you do this, I must obtain a new blade."

There, under the lilting orange leaves, the young warriors sit around a council stone. Ishida stands in his place at the clandestine meeting. He makes his case for the eight other young warriors to leave the Hotaru-Raikō and embark with him on his quest for power and glory. He uses the courtship to convince his fellow soldiers that the daimyō does not care about them. "We will never be given status or power while Takeda is daimyō. He does not appreciate our skills or prowess as samurai. This is why we are not even considered ashigaru yet. I think he fears us." He pauses. "But I have found one who has the power to place me in his stead." The others listen contemplatively. "When the time comes, I will need powerful samurai to control the Hotaru-Raikō. I ask you to follow me." He continues to stand in his place at the council, observing the others as they consider his request.

---

[23] Little girl (translated from Japanese).

One of the eight, Takayama, breaks the silence. "What you are asking us to do is wrong. Takeda-san is a just and fair lord. We owe him our loyalty, our swords—" Before he can finish speaking, Ishida, in a fluid motion and without warning, removes a tantō from his obi and slices Takayama's neck. He falls backward, dying as he does. The remaining seven are shocked by the swiftness of the assassination. They quickly understand disloyalty to Ishida will end in death. Their weak, fearful minds succumb to the strong will of their new leader. They agree to follow him, forever leaving their homes and their families.

"Tie a stone around Takayama's feet and throw him in the moat," Ishida commands as he removes Takayama's blades, taking them for his own. He then slices a piece of fabric from Takayama's clothes. "No hotaru must know our plans," he commands as he wipes the blood from his tantō. The rest quickly carry out his commands while Ishida stares down at the crimson-stained steel. Though free of blood, the cursed blade now glows red in the sunlight. The desire to hide his betrayal prompts him to quickly hide the blade in its sheath.

After they do their master's bidding, Ishida leads his new ashigaru south to the Kyoto Province. There, over the long winter months, Kumo will poison their minds and corrupt their bodies in service to her and her alone. Like the cursed blade of their treacherous leader, the light of their weapons and armor fades from a pale white to deep crimson.

Ishida's lust for Kumo and envy of Takeda twist his mind. His hair turns a light gray, like the color of Kumo's webs. And he lets it fall freely, never again putting it in a topknot. He keeps his face covered in public with a red devil's mask, his antennae sheltered in the protective horns of the mask. Kumo, using her silk and the husks of discarded beetles, weaves a new, jet-black armor for him. She ties a golden rope over the crimson obi around his waist. The shell plates of his armor are triangular in shape, sewn closely together, and overlap like that of a serpent's skin. The scales on his thigh armor are a bloodstained, reddish brown. He takes pleasure in the fear his appearance instills in those who come across him.

Ishida and his soldiers form Kumo's new Tsuchigumo clan. She declares herself kōgō[24] and gives the title of daimyō to Ishida. With the makings of this new clan, she introduces them to her kaijū,[25] who will be the general of her army. She lays out her plan to unleash a legion of fierce beasts just like him from the abyss. The kaijū will be one of many generals leading these beasts to plague man and slaughter her enemies.

She regales her clan with the story of how she conjured the kaijū, how it provided the location of the gate to their realm, hidden deep in the forest, in a long-forgotten shrine at the base of Hakusan. She tells them the Hotaru-Raikō are the only thing standing in her way. Therefore, Takeda and his samurai must be destroyed. All she needs now is the perfect opportunity to put her plans in action.

---

[24] Queen (translated from Japanese).
[25] Pronounced "k-eye-joo"—meaning "strange beast" (translated from Japanese).

CHAPTER 2

Unexpected Journey

Saitō visits Ashi almost daily for the next few weeks. On sunny afternoons, after his training is completed, they meet in the open-air pavilion. There they talk, stare at the distant Hakusan, and sometimes watch the moon rise. On rainy or cold days, they meet in the warmer and dryer tsuridono where he shares poetry with her, and she will occasionally play music for him. The light of their love grows brighter each passing day. Takeda and Harumi are both pleased with their budding romance and announce a spring wedding. They decree those preparations will begin at the first sign of the cherry blossom.

*****

Months pass. The days are growing longer, the sun warms the earth, the snows are melting, and all signs point to a waking nature. The moss on the shrine is turning a deeper green. The heavy wooden thicket has begun to bud, and the cherry tree blossoms are swelling. It is during an early morning walk in the niwa, inspecting the cherry tree with anticipation, that Ashi notices a light in the shrine above. Her father is there, speaking with a stranger. *It is much too early in the season for visitors*, she thinks. *Who could it be?* The stranger stands in the shadowy area of the old ishidōrō. The morning sun has not risen high enough to illuminate the shrine either. So, try as she might, she cannot make out the stranger's features. She conceals herself in the covered pavilion and quietly waits for a glimpse of the stranger when they come down the path.

Several minutes later, her father emerges from the shrine. He descends the path alone and in deep contemplation. Ashi looks back at the shrine, but it is empty. She waits patiently for her father to pass through the torii. "Good morning, Father," she calls sweetly.

Takeda-san stirs from his thoughts. "Ah, Ashi-himē," he replies. "My beautiful daughter."

Ever the bold one, Ashi asks him, "May I share in your thoughts?"

"Īe, not right now," he replies softly. "Iku.[26] Tell your mother we must all speak privately. I will meet you in the main hall."

Ashi scurries back up the rō to the shinden to inform her mother, Harumi. Together they prepare a miso soup to warm him. Takeda-san is grateful upon receiving it. They sit together and share their meal. Afterward, he lets them know the stranger in the shrine was a messenger from Tengoku. "I am to take two of my best samurai, along with two-thirds of our army, and immediately depart on a mission in a faraway land.[27] Also, and most regretfully, we must postpone your wedding, Ashi, until I return." He can see the disappointment in Ashi's eyes but continues on. "Harumi, I leave the

---

[26] Pronounced "Ee-kooh"—meaning "Go" (translated from Japanese).

[27] See *Guardian of the Lightning Seeds* for the full adventure.

25

Raikō estate in your hands. Ashi is of age and is well trained; she is onna-musha. We will test Saitō while I am away. He must suspend the search for the eight missing students. I will make him samurai and give him the east tainoya to reside in, and he will now serve as your liaison to the Hotaru no Chikyū."

"Hai," agrees Harumi. Though she understands and knows he will serve Kami faithfully, Harumi is saddened by the announcement. Something in her heart tells her she will not see him in this world again.

Ashi, studying her father's face, lets her emotions get the best of her. She uncharacteristically jumps up and runs to her chambers.

Stunned by her outburst, Takeda looks with some confusion at Harumi, who nods her head and humbly directs, "Iku, husband. She needs you. Comfort her."

He gets up slowly and walks quietly to her room. Stopping outside her chamber, he lets his shadow linger on the rice paper door. He can hear her crying and politely waits for Ashi to quiet herself. Once she is still, he slides the panel door open. She has collected herself and sits on her feet in the seiza position on her tatami mat. Her back is upright, and her hands are folded in the middle of her lap. She sits quietly with her right side facing the door. Takeda enters and sits on the mat directly across from her. "Daughter?" he inquires lovingly. "What troubles you?"

She looks into his eyes. "Please don't go, Papa. I have a terrible feeling about this mission." She breaks protocol, lunges, and wraps her arms around him.

"Ashi-himē," he begins as he returns her embrace, "I must go. This task comes from God himself. I dare not dishonor him. You must have faith that all is done according to his will." He pauses for a moment to gently pat and rub her back. "Your mother, gentle as she may be, is onna-musha; she will protect you with the ferocity of a mother fox for her kit. You also have Saitō now, who has proven himself worthy to this day. Besides—"

"I don't want to lose you," Ashi blurts out.

"Saiai no musume,[28] it will be okay. Do you remember why God sent us here? To this island, closed off to the rest of the world? I myself wondered that for many years. The men of this land are feudal and warlike at times, yet the divine law of God is written on their hearts. They see it in nature all around them, yet they don't yet know the Author of this law. They hold reason and morality on high pedestals and value the customs of their ancestors. I know Kami wanted us to learn from them, learn the way of the warrior so we might defend them against unseen evil in this land or"—he pauses as he again pats her gently on the back—"in faraway lands."

Ashi sits upright and stares deeply into her father's eyes. Her father continues to firmly, but gently, hold her shoulders for a moment. "You must remember, my daughter, I do not fear death. Neither should you. It is in death that we find our way…our way back to Kami. Dying for the Lord while fighting evil or protecting the weak is an honorable thing. Death is not to be feared. If it is my time, then I will gladly give my life for God, so I might not only bring him glory but honor to our family as well." Takeda releases her shoulders, sits back on his feet, and places his hands on his legs. "You must be courageous, Ashi. I know you will find the strength to protect our clan in my absence and to defend those who cannot defend themselves." He offers a humble yet reassuring smile. "And, God willing, we will return so that I may bless your marriage to Saitō."

---

[28] Beloved daughter (translated from Japanese).

"Hai," says Ashi, sniffling. She does her best to put on a brave appearance. "I will be strong for you, Father."

"Hrmm… I know you will, musume." Takeda takes his folded fan from his obi. "You always make me happy and proud. I will love you forever, in this world and in the next." He offers the kind of fatherly smile that goes straight to the heart and soul of a daughter. She smiles back at him and quickly bows her head. Confident she will be okay, he gently taps her on the knee with his closed fan before taking his leave.

Takeda returns to Harumi, who has finished cleaning the table. "All is better, my wife, but you will check on her later?" She smiles and bows her head slightly in agreement. "Yoi. I go to make arrangements for the mission." Takeda leaves the shinden, spending the rest of the day speaking with his samurai. Together, they gather his army and prepare for the journey. Ashi spends her day pouring all her love into the making of a single kanji, a gift for her father to take with him.

Ashi's mother comes to check in on her and finds her making the kanji. She does not disturb her daughter, rather she stands silently in the opening of the door watching her pour her love into its creation. A tear wells up in her eye when she gets a glimpse of the kanji. Harumi has always been proud of Ashi's exceptional ability to write so elegantly in both the masculine and feminine.

*****

The moment has come to say farewell. It is not, nor has it ever been, easy for Harumi to see her husband off to conflict. She, too, feels this might be the last time she is with her husband. Harumi gets up early the next morning, to help him don his armor. It is a solemn but serene moment shared between them. She begins by sliding his kosode over his arms, draping it on his shoulders from behind. She moves quietly, lovingly, around to fold it over in front of him. She does not look him in the eye but humbly and gracefully goes about her work.

Takeda looks down at this beautiful wife as she folds his kosode. He thinks back to long ago when he took Harumi as his wife after arriving in Nihon. As Saitō is drawn to Ashi, he too was drawn to Harumi's inner light. It is a gentle, soothing glow that captured and has kept his desire for hundreds of years. In their youth, they had many adventures, adventures that spanned most of the island nation of Nihon. Now, as a weathered daimyō and father, he relies on her to bring balance not only to his lordship of the clan but also within his own household. He knows he would be only a half-empty shell if he lost her. So it is in these quiet moments, when not a word is spoken, that he cherishes every touch of her hand as she slowly dresses him in the ornate armor. For Harumi, it is in this service that she shows her love and devotion to her faithful husband.

Later, the Hotaru-Raikō army assembles in the predawn glow, which illuminates the courtyard. Ashi awaits her father just inside the southern doors of the shinden leading out onto the covered veranda. She bows low as he approaches, her mother just behind him. She holds up a scroll of rice paper for him. He stops and looks down lovingly at her. He then tenderly takes the scroll and slowly unfurls it. The word 愛 (*Ai*, or "love") is delicately and beautifully scribed there. He scrolls the paper back up and returns her bow. She rises to see him. Takeda leans in and lightly kisses his beloved daughter on the forehead. Not a word is said; none is needed. Father, mother, and daughter all know their bond—a deep familial love and devotion, which is unbreakable. No matter what comes, the love they share can never be taken from them. Takeda-san moves to the doors. Mother and daughter each slide one side open, presenting the great leader to his army. He steps out onto the top step of the veranda. His samurai bow low followed by the assembled army, all in unison. The daimyō's heart swells with pride; he is inspired by the loyalty and confidence of his men. He offers a bow of gratitude in return. He then stands upright and lifts his wing covers horizontally. The white edge, which runs along each dark-brown cover, glints in the sunlight. His strong, smoke-colored wings unfurl in the rising sun. Emulating their master, the army also prepares for flight in unison. The drone of their wings fills the niwa. Without a word, Takeda-san rises into the air and heads east. His faithful army follows. They hold their heads up high, looking to the horizon with conviction.

*****

In the Kyoto Province, Kumo grows impatient. It has been a long winter, and her hatred of both man and hotaru has deepened. Long ago she was being driven north out of the Nara Prefecture. The men of Kyoto also discovered her true nature, causing her to flee even further north into the dense woods. Seeking revenge, she discovered a way to summon a single kaijū. This monster told her of a legion of others just like him, waiting in Abaddon to torment men and destroy their crops.

Now she sits on her throne of stag beetle husks, remembering its words, "They need only be released." Her spies have found the gate, her army is primed, and she is poised to release the devastating horde. Her long-awaited revenge is at hand; only the Hotaru-Raikō stand in her way. Kumo is overjoyed when word of the daimyō's absence finally reaches her. She is told two-thirds of their army have left Nihon. Their absence is the opportunity she has been looking for. She prepares her treacherous Tsuchigumo clan to travel to Hakusan where she will open the gate to the abyss.

*****

Spring and most of the summer have passed. Late summer heat is already giving way to cooler temperatures. A village subdued by the absence of its warriors sits quietly by the placid waters of the Fukui Castle moat. A familiar sound, faintly at first, begins to infiltrate from the east. The distinct sound of humming perks up the antennae of the denizens of the Raikō Village; they know that sound. The Hotaru-Raikō army returns. Villagers rush past the ishidōrō shrine to line the outer edges of the courtyard, eager to greet their fathers, sons, and brothers.

Keeping low to the ground, a steady stream of armored ashigaru follow their daimyō and his samurai. Takeda is used to a larger greeting when he returns from much shorter excursions. Surveying the inner lights of those who welcome his return, he senses both joy and sadness in them. He wonders if it is because they see the returning army's numbers are fewer or something has happened to his clansmen while they were away. Either way, something is wrong.

As soon as he sets his sandaled foot upon the gravelly courtyard, Takeda calls his samurai, Sasaki-san and Hatano-san, to him. Speaking quietly to them, he states, "Something is amiss. There is an unsettled feeling among our people. Discover what has taken place in our absence." He pauses as he notices the widow of Hasegawa[29] seeking her fallen husband among the soldiers. "Speak with the widows and children of the fallen. We must care for them in their mourning and provide for them in their need. My wealth is theirs. I would ensure they have anything they need."

Both men discretely exclaim, "Hai!" They reunite with their own families before going on to investigate what has transpired in their absence and consoling the families of the fallen.

Folding his wings under their hard shell, Takeda-san turns toward his home. Ashi is standing on the top step of the veranda, looking down at him with a longing. He knows his daughter. He reads many things in her eyes; there is a relief and joy in his return, but there is also a sadness. Ashi is holding back tears of distress, of a heavy burden. He knows she wishes to run to him but is restraining herself. Indeed, something bad has happened. Takeda looks around for Harumi, too, but quickly realizes she is nowhere to be seen. He walks toward the steps and greets her, "Kon'nichiwa, Ashi-himē. I have missed you, daughter." He stops at the top step and faces her. "Where is your mother? Why does she not come out to greet me?"

"Father," she begins, "I have grave news." Ashi is losing the fight to hold back her emotions. "Come inside so I may tell you." She bows, turns, and slides the door open for him to enter. Takeda enters, and Ashi quickly closes the door behind them. Seeking the security of her father's arms, she surprises him with an embrace. It is tender and heartfelt; Takeda returns it unreservedly. Comforted, she finally pulls back.

Takeda looks deep into her eyes. "Where is your mother?"

---

[29] Learn about Hasegawa in *Guardian of the Lightning Seeds*.

"Oh, Papa, Mother went to one of the onsen[30] on Hakusan to search for kuro yuri[31] weeks ago. Neither she nor her escort ever returned. I've been doing my best to keep everyone's spirits high, but the whole village knows she is missing. They fear the worst."

A sense of urgency wells up in Takeda's chest. He tells Ashi, "Hang lanterns all around the niwa to help light her way back, just in case. Where is Saitō? Has he treated you well?"

"Hai, Papa, he has. He has brought much honor upon our house during your absence. He should be coming back from a visit with King Hi-marō and the Hotaru no Chikyū soon."

"Yoi. Send him to me as soon as he returns. Tomorrow I will take him and a squad of fresh ashigaru to find your mother." He begins to walk toward his chamber. Ashi follows him closely. "While we search, I want to you to work with the other wives and daughters to prepare a small festival for the returning army. We will share the details of our journey then." He stops, faces Ashi, and stares lovingly at his daughter. "It will give you something to do, Ashi, and will take your mind off your troubles and reassure our people." He offers a comforting smile.

"Hai, Otousan."[32] She knows he is right.

"Now, I really must bathe and put on fresh clothes." Takeda-san heads into his chamber and slides the door shut behind him. He hears his daughter rush off. Knowing he is finally alone, he sighs quietly. His already heavy heart sinks further into his chest, but he has never been one to give into sadness. He removes his armor, bathes, and then puts on fresh

---

[30] Hot springs (translated from Japanese).
[31] A rare, chocolate-colored lily that grows on the slopes of Mount Haku.
[32] Father (translated from Japanese).

clothes. He knows prayer is needed and goes discretely into the shrine to not only give thanks for those who returned with him but also pray for his lost wife.

Ashi sends Saitō to meet her father in the shrine. Saitō eagerly wants to give a full account of all that has happened when he arrives, but Takeda-san informs him of the following day's mission instead and his role in it. "I understand you have brought honor upon my house, Saitō-san. You have made me proud. I look forward to hearing all that has happened while we travel tomorrow. For now, though, iku. Find Sasaki-san and Hatano-san. Send them to me here, in the shrine."

"Hai!" answers Saitō before bowing and carrying out his lord's orders.

While he waits, Takeda prays and meditates. His heart and mind are burdened by much: the loss of so many fine soldiers in the faraway land, his missing wife, and now an overwhelming sense of betrayal from someone within his own clan. Again, the sense of urgency to find his beloved, and the truth of what has happened, fills him.

His loyal samurai join him a short while later. Though deep in contemplative prayer, Takeda knows when they arrive; he can feel their presence. He trusts only God and his family more than them. Sasaki and Hatano have entered quietly and respectfully wait until he is finished. Without opening his eyes, he asks of them, "What have you discovered?"

"Masutā, there are rumors of an unseen evil moving through the woods. The eight students never returned, nor were their bodies ever found. Much suspicion surrounds their disappearance. It is even whispered they travel with the wicked shadow," informs Hatano-san.

"Hrmmpf," grunts Takeda. He says only one word, a name, "Ishida." He reflects on what Ashi told him about the greed and lust, the dimming of Ishida's light, she saw in the market last year. Takeda wonders if he is the source of this sense of betrayal he feels. "Select a squad of fresh soldiers. They will accompany Saitō with me on a search party tomorrow morning." The daimyō opens his eyes and looks at his samurai. "Sasaki-san, Hatano-san, we will search for four days. You have earned the time to rest. Iku. Spend time with your families while we are away, but be on alert." Both samurai say thank you and then get up to leave. "Hatano-san."

"Hai, sensei."

"Kudasai,[33] send your daughter, Yui, to keep Ashi company while she prepares for the festivities."

"Hai." Hatano-san need not ask why; he understands his master. He leaves silently while Takeda closes his eyes and returns to prayer.

*****

The next morning, Takeda-san leads Saitō and a squad of soldiers on the long journey to the two hot springs at the base of Hakusan. Though it is a lengthy trip, Takeda relishes being back in Nihon, flying through the lush forests surrounding the mountain. He reflects on memories of gliding up the mountain with his beloved Harumi. Back then, before Ashi was born, they would playfully weave and dance around the beech, mizunara, and tochinoki trees. The smell of rain-soaked leaves and pine needles would fill his nostrils, while the warmth of sun beams passing through gaps in the leafy canopy overhead would warm his body. Today he is motivated by something different, a concern for his bride.

During the summer months, vast amounts of flowers bloom simultaneously on Hakusan's open mountainsides.

---

[33] Please (translated from Japanese).

Though he knows those blooms will be fading now, he longs to look upon those fields again and remember the first time he and Harumi emerged into the open-air meadows. Amazingly fragrant breezes would waft down from the summit. He recalls the awe-filled expression upon Harumi's face, the brightness of her eyes, the first time they flew out over the sprawling fields. The shear sight of the colorful glade was one of the few places he could even remotely compare anything on earth to what he knew of heaven. He delighted in watching his bride dip, dive, and waltz among those blooms. She danced all the way up into the sparser alpine fields, stopping only to breathe deep of the small, delicate white and lavender hakusanfuro flowers, the deep-purple, daisy-like hakusankozakura flowers with their yellow hearts, and, his favorite, gozen-tachibana. Though their blossoms are waning, the beauty of what still blooms is not lost on him, or his soldiers, as they reach the alpine meadows.

He looks for the gozen-tachibana flower, which grows in clusters and is made of four small and delicate white petals surrounded by five or six pointy and verdant leaves. He is inspired by the beautiful floral star, but that is not why it is his favorite though. It is his favorite because it produces a sweet, delicious, bright-red berry he likes to pluck and eat. This day, the flowers are sparse though, and the berries have not quite ripened. The joy of nibbling on berries is not to be. His empty stomach growls at his heavy heart as the search of his lost bride continues.

They fly north and east to the Ichirino onsen first, hoping maybe they will find her stranded there. Instead, they find no trace. They camp there for the night before traveling south to the spring near the small human village of Shiramine the next morning. There, inspecting the area around the onsen, one of the soldiers spots a piece of material. A tattered cloth torn from a robe clings to the broken branch of a shrub. The soldier collects it and hurriedly brings it to his master who instantly recognizes the material. It belonged to Harumi, an uchigi he had given her years ago. He is devastated. The mountainside is silent; he hears only the wind blow. The depressing silence is pierced by the screech of a golden eagle in the quiet summer sky. He looks up to see the bird soaring in the pale-blue heavens overhead. He thinks of his "big brother" Hania, in the faraway land, and wonders if the bird is an omen or warning.

They begin to thoroughly examine the surrounding area. Not far from the onsen, they find a strange, oblong object covered in webs. It looks like the remains of a spider's discarded prey, but it is too large. Saitō approaches cautiously, removes his tantō, and slices through the web. He takes a step back; he is shocked at what he sees. All that remains is the husk of one of his fellow Hotaru-Raikō. The body, withered and distorted, fills only half of the armor encased in the webbing. All the fluids have been drained from the victim, giving him a mummified appearance. Saitō covers his mouth and nose while sheathing his blade. "What could have done this, my lord?" He looks to Takeda-san who also inspects the body. "There is no spider large enough to attack us in this way. What else could have done this?"

The daimyō breaks a stick off the nearby bush. He pokes at a black, tar-like substance next to the body. He scrapes at it with the stick, but it does not dissipate over the rock. It reminds him of spittle.

"Over here, my lord. We found another," calls another soldier. Several feet away, one more cocooned body is found.

"This must be the other escort," states Saitō. He sees the desperation and anger rising in his master's face. He motions to the others. "Spread out! Keep looking for our lady."

"Saitō," says Takeda in a deep voice.

"Hai, masutā."

"Have two ashigaru burn these bodies. We will continue the search and then collect their bones for burial later."

"Hai," Saitō obeys. He passes the orders to two soldiers who set the bodies alight where they lie. He then joins the rest in searching for Lady Harumi. Takeda-san stands tall, one hand on his sword handle, slowly scanning the rocky mountain, the swaying meadows, and the edge of the forest. He looks for signs of enemy movement or the haunting presence of yūrei.[34]

They search for a couple of hours while the bodies of the escorts are cremated but find no sign of Lady Harumi. Takeda recalls his troops from their search and tasks them with collecting any remaining bones of the dead so they may have a proper burial in their village cemetery. He moves up the mountainside to a rock outcropping, away from his troops. There, among the alpine flowers, he kneels in reflection and prayer. He remembers coming here years ago, relaxing in the warm waters while watching Harumi bathe. Takeda closes his eyes. He can still see water glisten on her soft, milky-white skin and her smile as she washed her jet-black hair in the hot spring waters. Instead of joy however, the memory brings him sadness. He can feel the loss of her light in the world. He knows deep down his wife's fate has been sealed by whomever, or whatever, did this. He prays to Kami for the soul of his wife and her escorts. He gives thanks for keeping Ashi and the rest of the village safe in his absence. Lastly, he asks God for justice, for the destruction of those who would kill in such a deviant and cowardly way. The daimyō returns to his troops afterward and then leads them back home.

---

[34] Ghosts or spirits (translated from Japanese).

The expedition returns to find Ashi and Yui have orga-
nized a wonderful feast. Saitō takes the bones of the fallen
to the village priest, while Takeda goes silently to his shinden, speaking to no one. Ashi visits her father immediately
after his arrival. She is the only one outside his expedition
who learns the sad news. Though he truly loves his daughter,
he gently asks her to leave. "Kudasai, musume, spend some
time with Saitō; be with the one you love before you have to
turn in for the night. You will need all the sleep you can get
for tomorrow's festivities." He then walks contemplatively
through the western rō and into the private pavilion. From
there he slips outside and goes up into the shrine for medi-
tation. He stays until he is exhausted and then turns in for a
restless sleep.

*****

The next morning the daimyō leads a procession of
samurai, elders, and priests into the shrine to place the medi-
cine wheel he received from Hania on the altar. There he also
reveals the sad news that Lady Harumi has been lost. "We
will mourn her together tomorrow." He proclaims, "Today,
let us rejoice in those who returned from our distant journey
and honor those who gave their lives in service to Kami."
Ashi joins him in leading everyone down into the courtyard.
There they preside over the festival.

The returning warriors act out a play depicting the journey with the young Notah who becomes Hania. They tell
the story of how Hasegawa earned his new name, "Wrestles
with Hare," and the honorable way he died. The troupe also
performs a reenactment of the battle to retrieve the lightning
seeds. Joy, laughter, and a deep sense of filial pride return to
the whole village. After the play, a few of the young warriors

compete in Sumai no Sechi for their daimyō, who watches with a saddened heart and burdened mind. Hiding these emotions, he not only congratulates the winners but fulfils his duty to his people by offering the much-needed festival. They, in return, prepare for the dance to honor the spirits of their dead. It is during the dance that Takeda-san sees something, which brings him hope and happiness.

Saitō respectfully approaches Ashi, who sits near her father, and offers a low bow to them both. The daimyō gives an approving smile and bow. Even though Takeda knows Ashi mourns the loss of her mother, he witnesses both of their lights brighten when Saitō reaches for her hand. From his seat overlooking the festival, a father watches his daughter dance with her betrothed. Their bodies flash and glow with a brilliant radiance. Truly he can see the bond, the love they share. The strong and deep connection between them brings him peace. As a father and a lord, Takeda-san knows he has chosen the right samurai to marry Ashi and is looking forward to grooming him to take over the clan one day.

The entire village enjoys feasting, games, and uplifting times well into the evening. Night settles in, and most slip into a restful night's sleep. A serene hush settles over the quaint village…until the early morning hours. Sometime around three, the distant sound of taiko drums is heard, echoing through the woods like far-off thunder. Muffled by a light fog, the rhythmic beats are faint at first but grow louder and faster. They wake Takeda and his samurai. There is a ferocity, a malevolence, in their tone; it puts village guards on edge. Then, before the location of the drums can be determined, they fall silent. Like the cry of the golden eagle on the previous day, the lord of the Hotaru-Raikō knows the drums are a foreboding sign.

CHAPTER 3

Death of the Samurai

After the drumming stops, Takeda-san immediately calls for his samurai. He also sends runners to consult the guards around Raikō Village and discern from which direction the sounds came. They all come back to the steps in front of the shinden. Takeda-san stands on the top step with Saitō on his left and Ashi by the doors behind him.

"The eastern guards report the drums seemed to be coming from the base of Hakusan, masutā," informs Sasaki.

Hatano reports, "The northern guards saw no activity in Fukui Castle, my lord. This means the sound was not in the frequency of man's hearing."

"Hmmpf. Am I to have no peace?" grumbles an exhausted Takeda. "Sasaki-san, Hatano-san, prepare two squads of ashigaru. We will investigate the drums." The two samurai bow and immediately run to prepare.

"And me, lord?" inquires Saitō as he steps closer.

"Go to your tainoya. Prepare your armor. You will go with us."

"Hai," Saitō responds with eagerness.

Takeda-san turns to face his daughter. "Ashi, you are onna-musha. I leave the defense of the clan to you. I pray, daughter, that it will not be needed."

"Hai. Me, too, Father." She opens the door for him as he strides in her direction.

*****

One of the eastern guards is among the ten warriors who gather in the niwa later. Since he heard from which direction the drums came, he will be their scout. The samurai inspect the men and make sure they are ready for battle while they wait for their daimyō. He emerges and, without hesitation, takes to the sky. The band of warriors quickly follow him out into the chilly morning air. Their brightly glowing armor and sashimono are striking against the black, predawn landscape. In the distance overhead, yellow fades to orange, then purple, blue, and finally the fading night sky. Ashi moves out onto the veranda. She watches the white lights move quickly toward Hakusan before disappearing in the wooded distance. She goes back in to dress in her formal attire and once again fulfil her leadership role in the village.

*****

It is midday, and Takeda is growing weary. The lack of sleep. The heartbreak. Continually searching in vain for the missing. He has only had a single day's rest. Death and ominous signs of something wicked are everywhere without any trace of who or what is causing it. He does his best to remain disciplined, to keep striving forward with what he believes to be the right course.

Today, his Hotaru-Raikō search the northern section of the Kuzuryu River basin, all the way up to where it meets the Takinami River. From there, they move to the east of the confluence to the foot of the mountains. There is an area where bones of ancient, prehuman beasts can be spotted. Takeda knows of a large beech tree to rest in near the site and leads his men there. All are happy to rest in the shade of the lush tree. They sip nectar from the lotus and nibble on the seeds from the flower's pods.

Resting on a branch further up from his ashigaru, Takeda hears the distinct screech from a golden eagle in the distant sky. He looks up just in time to see a barrage of arrows raining down upon them. He sounds the alarm, but it is too late. Half of his warriors are slain by the volley of arrows. Saitō, Sasaki, Hatano, and the remaining warriors draw their swords and fly up to surround their daimyō. Fierce howls and screams fill the air around them. Creatures resembling their own kind, yet twisted, buzz through the air, cutting down every surviving Hotaru-Raikō. Hatano steps out on the branch desperately trying to get a good look at the enemy but is cut down by a blur and a flash of red light. His limp body falls to the unyielding ground below. Everyone—save Saitō, Sasaki, and Takeda—has fallen from the tree.

Takeda stands with his back to the tree, while his remaining samurai hover just in front and to the left and right of him. The enemy disappears as fast as it came. An unsettling quiet permeates the shadowy canopy. Swords drawn, the three warriors keep their guard up. There is silence, an eerie stillness. Then they hear noise, something large crashing down through the canopy. A huge locust, longer than they are and just as tall in height as the Hotaru-Raikō, breaks through the leaves. It lands on the branch in front of Takeda with a thud. Its appearance is grotesque. A black, ink-like saliva drips from the sharp teeth protruding from his almost human-looking face. Takeda watches the saliva land on the branch, and he recognizes the consistency; it is the same as he found at the onsen. A wrath rises in his chest. "Monsutā!"[35] he screams, holding the tip of his sword outward toward the beast. Its white blade glows bright as lightning in the shade of the beech tree. "You took my beloved from me!"

The locust lets out a guttural laugh as he opens his wing covers. His red-tinged wings begin to beat, and he rises slowly into the air, hovering just over the branch. Takeda does not hesitate. He begins to charge, running along the branch. His eyes are locked onto the monster's. Unfortunately, he does not see the scorpion-like tail uncurling from its back. Sasaki does see it from his position. He flies quickly in front of his lord to cut the tail, but he is not fast enough. Instead, the barb of the tail runs completely through Sasaki's abdomen, and its tip pierces Takeda's chest, injecting its venom into the daimyō. The monster whips his tail backward, discarding the samurai to the ground while watching the reaction of his true target.

The light of Takeda's sword dims as he stumbles and begins to fall from the branch. Saitō swoops to his aid, catches him in midair, and begins to fly downward, away from the tree and down toward the river. An arrow from an unseen enemy in the tree is loosed; it goes through Saitō's wing but misses its true mark. The pain is agonizing, but he sputters on toward the water. Once over the river, he turns his body so that his unconscious master is above him, painfully folds his wings under their covers, and freefalls, plunging into the Takinami River.

The enemy loses sight of them, but it matters not to them. "They're dead, or soon will be," comes a sultry voice

---

[35] Monster (translated from Japanese).

from the shadows in the trees. "Gather the bodies of the fallen beneath the tree. They can still serve me in death."

*****

Three days pass, and Ashi fears neither her father nor her betrothed will return. Near the evening of the third day, Saitō is spotted by guards carrying her father over his shoulders toward the eastern gate. He is on foot. And one of his wings, damaged from the arrow, is sticking out from under its cover, dragging in the dirt. The guards announce their approach. Ashi, accompanied by other warriors, runs out to meet them.

"Your father…" starts Saitō, he himself desperate for breath, "he is wounded…poisoned. Quickly, take him." The guards take their unresponsive daimyō and rush toward the shinden. Saitō, walking next to Ashi and dragging his feet, does not reach the courtyard. He collapses to the ground from exhaustion after passing through the outer gate. He is battered, bruised, and breathing heavily. Villagers come to help carry him to the eastern tainoya.

Once inside, servants immediately attend to Takeda-san. They remove his armor, bathe him, dress his wound, and clothe him in a new kosode before placing him in his bed. The poison has taken its toll; there is nothing they can do to save him. Ashi stays with Saitō for a short time while they care for her father. She helps treat his wounded wing while he tells her about being ambushed and about the monster that poisoned her father. He explains how they escaped and, using a lily pad as a raft, floated down the Kuzuryu River to Eiheiji. From there they traveled the rest of the way on foot. Ashi can see he is exhausted. She calms him and quickly gets him to rest. As soon as he is asleep, she leaves to be with her father.

Ashi enters his room, and all the attendants leave. She quietly slides the door shut and then immediately kneels at his side. With her hands clasped together on her lap, she leans down to his ear and whispers, "Papa?"

Her father barely opens his eyes. He groans in agony as he turns his head slightly to see her. "Saiai…no musume," he labors to say. "I… I love…"—his voice trails off to a mere whisper—"you…" He exhales. Closing his eyes, he breathes his last.

Ashi stares down at him, stunned. She leans over his body, resting her head on his chest. Tears stream uncontrollably down her soft cheeks. She wants more time with her father. She does not know what to do or what to say; she just cries. It takes a couple of minutes, but she forces herself from her sorrow and sits back up. She lovingly turns his head, so he is facing skyward. She kisses his cheek and, through her tears, whispers, "Go in peace, Otousan. May you find Mother waiting for you in the fields of Tengoku."

Ashi feels lost, alone. Her mother is assumed dead, her body never recovered. Her father has been killed by an assassin, and her betrothed lies injured down the hall. Their warrior ranks have been decimated. Standing, she collects herself. *I promised Father I would be strong,* she thinks. *I must honor my parent's memory.* She leaves her father's room and walks stoically toward the niwa. Sadness tugs her heart lower. Ashi covers her head with her uchigi, wrapping it around her so only her face shows as she walks out into the night air. She looks up to the long band of twinkling stars set against the dark sky. She lets out an unconscious sigh and then steps out into the empty, gravel courtyard.

Although she loves Saitō, her thoughts dwell upon her father. Ashi walks aimlessly, desperately trying to collect her feelings and process everything that has happened. *So many dead.* The burden of leadership in such a desperate time falls squarely upon her shoulders. *So many expectations. I never anticipated to be without my father's guidance so soon. How can I lead the Hotaru-Raikō now? Must we move again? We still don't know the source of the drums or the magnitude of what we face. How can we defeat the unknown?* She selfishly wonders if it would have been better to have perished with her mother and father. *There is so much uncertainty about what is to come,* she ponders.

Ashi is so deep in her thoughts she does not realize she has instinctively walked to the shrine entrance. She stops and looks up at the gakuzuka[36] on the faded wood torii. Carved in the wooden sign is the kanji 私, which translates to *Watashi* (or "I am"). A memory comes flooding into her mind, a memory from when she was a little shōjo. Her father once brought her up to the base of Hakusan on a Sunday. They sat together on a branch in a beech tree, looking up at the mountain and waiting for the sun to rise. She loved those moments with him. She loved that he never withheld his knowledge from her, especially regarding God. Again, his words return to her…

"Kami cannot be contained in a single shrine, Ashi-himē. All of nature is a shrine to him, a place to discover his creative majesty. Our humble shrine only helps us focus our thoughts on him and…"—he paused to look down and smile at her—"it helps us teach you and the other children about him." He exhaled as he turned his eyes back to the coming sunrise. "I cannot describe what it is like to be in Kami's presence. I do not possess the words for such magnificence, such feeling of awe and love." He was silent for a moment. "Beautiful though they are, even the elaborate tea

---

[36] Rectangular tablet in the top middle of a torii containing the name to whom the temple is dedicated (translated from Japanese).

ceremonies held in our shrine cannot compare with taking tea in Tengoku either." He silently reflected on the growing amber light from the rising sun. "Hrm… I must say I miss that tea too."

"They have tea in heaven, Papa?" asked little Ashi.

"Hai, musume. It is made from the leaves of the tree of life. We brewed the most delicious tea from the leaves that fell from it." He looked over at Ashi and winked. "This is what gives us our long lives." He returned his gaze to the rising sun. "Unfortunately, it was our quest for the perfect cup of tea that also led to our banishment to earth. In our pride, we decided to make a shimmering, white tea from new leaves still growing on the tree of life. What we did not understand at the time was that it was God who caused the leaves to fall, like ripened fruit, for us. There was always just enough for tea." Her father let out a sad sigh. "We had no right to pluck still growing leaves from the tree. We dishonored God by taking what was his and not respecting the gift he already gave us. And so, because of our pride and greed, he sent us to live here in Nihon until we are either redeemed by his Son or die in his service."

He reached over and gently tapped her on the leg with his folded fan. "Unfortunately, daughter, because you were born in this world, it will be harder for you, and all our ancestors, to maintain faith in our Creator. I am certain there will be challenging times when you will question your belief. When those times come, you must be still. You must seek him out in the beauty of his creation… You need only be calm and observe." He pointed his fan tip toward the brilliant golden light just starting to pierce the sky over the mountain peak. She remembers being dazzled by the rays of the rising sun reaching into the sky, embracing the heavens.

The light cresting the ridgeline that morning was so bright she could not look directly at it. Young Ashi closed her eyes. It has been years since. Now, as an adult, she opens them to a dark night. She is alone and dismayed. She mumbles to herself, "Where is the beauty now, Papa?"

Just then, something catches her eye. Ashi looks past the torii, up the path leading to the old ishidōrō shrine. Someone is standing there, near the entrance, someone she does not recognize—a tall, strong man wearing a pale-blue kataginu over a soft-gray kosode with gray hakama.[37] On his head is a bright tan sandogasa, the edge of its brim glowing with a white light all the way around it. The crest on his kataginu, a simple trinitarian symbol with a circle around it ⊛, also glows with a white light. Ashi recognizes it as a symbol of Kami, the one true God. The samurai stands, his hands in his sleeves, motionless in front of the shrine, staring down at Ashi as if expecting her.

She wonders if this is the same stranger who visited her father a few months earlier. Although it is a time of uncertainty and sorrow, Ashi is compelled by an overriding sense of duty. She subtly wipes any remaining tears from her youthful cheeks and pushes her fear and grief aside. She lets her uchigi down to her shoulders and stands upright. She changes the expression on her face to one of authority. It is her responsibility to find out who this visitor is. She starts up the path.

He removes his hands from his sleeves and holds them just above his waist, palms outward toward her. Though his appearance is stoic and stern, his voice is calming as he greets her, "Peace be upon you, young Ashi."

She bows and greets him, "Konbanwa.[38] How do you know me, sir?"

---

[37] Pleated and divided skirt (translated from Japanese).
[38] Good evening (translated from Japanese).

"All will be revealed in due time. Please, join me." The visitor invites Ashi into the shrine with a motion of his hand. Although he is a stranger, she looks deeply into his eyes and senses a profound holiness. She glances into the shrine and notices a black iron teapot with steaming water inside, a long bamboo ladle, and two tea bowls on the stone altar. Guarded, she bows again and then enters the shrine. The visitor follows her, removing his sandogasa as he enters. He takes a seat in front of the low stone altar where the flame for the old ishidōrō once burned. Ashi sits in the seiza position across from him. Wasting no time, the stranger reaches into his kosode, removes a tiny silk bag, opens it, and upends it over the teapot. A single gray leaf falls into the pot of steaming hot water. The stranger replaces the bag into his kosode. He smiles at her before saying, "We have much to discuss, Ashi-himē."

"I must know, How do you know me?"

"My name is Præsidiel. I was with your father during his recent journey to the distant lands." While the tea steeps, he reveals the true nature of his being and that he is a servant and messenger of God. He confirms it was he who visited her father and called him to action. Ashi sits in silent contemplation. Although she understands all he has said is truth, she still feels a numbness in her soul. Præsidiel senses this. He reaches for the teapot and slowly pours the tea into each of their cups. Ashi watches the vapor waft from the bowl with a trance-like stare; she can smell its delicate scent. Præsidiel picks up a cup and sets it down in front of her. "This will help," he says with a reassuring smile.

Ashi politely takes the cup; it is warm in her hands. She brings it to her lips and breathes deep of the rich, leafy aroma before quietly sipping it. She feels it trickle down her throat all the way to her stomach. Its warmth spreads out into her chest first and then to the rest of her body. Præsidiel hides a smile behind his own bowl as he watches her; he can see the light of peace return to her face. She slowly finishes her tea and returns her cup to the low altar. "Arigatou gozaimasu,"[39] she says humbly.

"You are most welcome, Ashi-himē." The angel also places his bowl down. "You know"—he smiles slyly—"your father loves this tea. It is his favorite. He is probably drinking some right now." She looks at him with much curiosity. "Yes, yes. Although his body was broken in this world, your father's spirit, his soul, is still very much alive." He pauses, leans toward her, and looks deep into her dark, almond-shaped eyes. "Everything he taught you about God and heaven is true. Keep this faith alive in your heart, and you will see both him and your mother again one day. I promise."

Tears well up in her eyes. Ashi, having no words to offer, places her hands, palm down, on the ground in front of her knees and offers the angel a low respectful bow as a way of saying thank you for the message. She lingers there a little longer than normal before slowly sitting upright again.

"It is written," informs Præsidiel, "the leaves of the tree of life are for the healing of nations." He sits upright and continues in a more authoritative voice, "To that end, I will leave a small amount of tea in the pot for you. When we have finished our discussion, you will take it to Saitō, pour it into a cup, and have him drink from it. The tea will heal his wing and restore his strength."

"Hai," she acknowledges softly.

"Now, for the other reason I have been sent. The spider yōkai, Kumo." The angel's face turns very serious. "She has recruited Ishida and others from your clan, seven of the missing students. She has already managed to call upon one of

---

[39] Thank you (translated from Japanese).

51

the foul creatures from the abyss. It is his poison that struck down your father. Her Tsuchigumo assassinated his samurai and ashigaru, as well as your mother. Now she seeks to release an entire horde of monsters, like the one that killed your father, upon the world. These creatures must *not* be released until the appointed time, by the designated emissary," he says with authority. "Kumo is overconfident. She thinks she has eliminated your most powerful warriors, but she does not know about you. She underestimates your people." He smiles at her. "You will lead two squads to the Shrine of Ancient Behemoths. There you must defeat Kumo and Ishida's traitorous Tsuchigumo, destroy the creature who escaped the abyss, and raze the shrine to the ground, forever sealing the gate there." The angel's tone softens a bit. "This is your purpose, onna-musha, to not only protect your clan and the inhabitants of Nihon but the whole world. Will you accept the will and tasking of God?"

"Hai. It will be done, mighty one."

"Your father has taught you well, Ashi. If you are successful, Kami will bless you and your people with peace." Præsidiel breathes deep and then exhales. "As is your custom, cremate your father's body and bury his bones tomorrow. Then give your people two days to mourn. You must depart on the third day. Saitō will lead you to the tree where your father was attacked. From there you can pick up the trail to the hidden torii. This is all I have to tell you." The angel stands. Ashi follows suit. She bows low to him out of respect, and he returns her bow. He turns and exits the shrine. As he places his sandogasa back upon his head, great white wings unfold from his shoulder blades. They are much larger than her own and are feathery. Looking over his shoulder, he offers Ashi, who is still standing just inside the shrine, a final piece of advice. "Those who overcome tribulation with faith in our

Lord earn the right to eat from the tree of life." He smiles one last time before taking flight into the dark starlit sky.

*****

Following the angel's direction, Ashi gives the tea to Saitō right after he departs. While he recovers the next morning, she cleans her father's armor and returns it to his gusoku bitsu.[40] Although his sword was lost in the river, she still has his wakizashi. She spends the morning inside her shinden cleaning, polishing, and placing it on a stand near his armor. She then prepares her jūnihitoe for the funeral. She steps back to look at it, and it triggers a more recent memory of her father.

It was only a couple of years ago, she recalls, when she was going about the castle grounds in a single white kosode, without more formal layers. This is unusual, even a bit cheeky, for a young princess. She was out in the courtyard when she heard her father's voice from the veranda. "Musume!" he called firmly but without anger. "Kudasai, come here." He was standing at the top step of the veranda with a folded cloth in his hands. She obediently ran to him and stood in the gravel at the bottom of the steps. "What are you doing out here in just your kosode?" he asked. Ashi had no reply. She turned her head downward in shame. "You are the daughter of the daimyō," instructed her father. "You are expected to dress in a more formal jūnihitoe." He moved down to the last step and said lovingly, "I have something for you."

Her father unfolded the silken orange and white uchigi with ornate tea leaf designs. After giving it a shake in the summer air, he cloaked her in it. Ashi happily pulled it around

---

[40] Armor display box with stand (translated from Japanese).

herself. Takeda-san also produced the obi that went with it. He wrapped it around her and tied it properly. "Turn," he directed. As gentle as a father can, he untucked her long, black hair so it cascaded down her back, standing out against the orange silk. She turned back to face him. Gently adjusting her beauty strands, he said, "Oh, one more thing." He pulled out an elaborate fan and presented it to her. "So you can maintain you modesty in public." Ashi opened the fan and brought it up to cover her mouth. "You are beautiful, my daughter," he remarked lovingly, a soft glow of fatherly affection in his eye. "Come. Let's go to the market."

Ashi remembers their slow walk through the niwa, past the shrine, and out into the village. As they did, her father affectionately taught her, "You are grown now, Ashi-himē. You must remember your station as my daughter, as onna-musha, and, along with your mother, as caretaker of our estate. Always carry yourself with dignity wherever you go." It was in those walks with him that she always learned and was comforted. She loved walking by his side through the village, visiting with all the Hotaru-Raikō. Today though, she makes ready for the long sad walk to the shrine behind his body.

In the early afternoon, Ashi-himē leads the procession of villagers through the torii and up the stone path to the old ishidōrō. They follow the body of her father, who is carried by his faithful retainers. Many Hotaru no Chikyū have come to pay their respects as well. They sit inside delicate paper lanterns lining the shrine's upward path, offering a mellow golden-yellow light in mourning of the noble daimyō and all who protect them.

Upon reaching the entrance to the shrine, she notices all the names of the fallen warriors have been scribed on wooden plates and hung in the corners of the immaculate shrine. A single hemp rope hangs over the stone table in the middle of the shrine. At the center of the rope hang two kanji, boldly scribed in black ink on white rice paper. They say 耶穌基督 (*Yē Sū Jī Dū*[41]). On the left side of the two kanji is the alpha character, and on the right is the omega (Ω) symbol. Ashi slowly and somberly approaches the stone table at the center. She places her father's lightless wakizashi there, carefully pointing the blade tip to the left. She kneels at the stone table, and the musicians begin to play softly. Though she is sad, the music brings her peace as she prays for both of her parents.

Ashi genuinely loved her mother, but there is something about the father–daughter relationship she already misses. Although he was tough, even strict at times, he was always patient with her. He could always boost her spirits when she was down. An excellent teacher, her father taught her a great deal about nature and how to live with others. Currently though, she thinks specifically of her father's teachings about heaven.

She was born in this world; she did not know Tengoku like her father. He would sometimes regale her with stories of heavenly life during their walks through town or when they flew among the trees. He would sometimes stop, look up past the brim of his favorite sandogasa, and stare into the deep-blue summer sky. "You must learn to live each moment of life, Ashi, to make it worthy." He often lamented being able to sip tea in the soft grass under the tree of life, remarking, "Although the tea in this world could never compare with the tea of heaven, it is in the company of your mother that I see Tokoma no Hara."[42] He loved making her mother smile regularly, and even blush sometimes, in a playful way of course.

---

[41] Jesus Christ (translated from Japanese).
[42] The plain of high heaven (translated from Japanese).

As she prays, Ashi remembers what he taught her about Tokoma no Hara and the vertical order of realms. "You must know the truth of these things, Ashi-himē. Men of Nihon often see the angels and the yōkai as gods themselves, but they are not. There is only one true God. Angels are the servants of God, and you must always respect them and fear their power; however, they are not to be worshiped. The yōkai are like Akuma, the first to fall. Like him they do want to be worshiped as God. They refuse to serve Kami; rather, they wish to supplant him. Tokoma no Hara is where heaven is, and I hope we all meet there again one day. Here, in Nakatsukumi,[43] you will be tested. And Yomi no Kuni, the world below, is where the enemies of God are sent."

Ashi prays to God, "I know you will give us justice, Lord. Let me be the instrument of your vengeance. Grant me the strength I need to destroy this evil, to send those who perpetrate it to Yomi no Kuni. Use me to bring peace and safety to my people and to protect man. Grant me courage to face our enemies. I humbly ask for these things in your name, Lord."

---

[43] The natural world we live in (translated from Japanese).

CHAPTER 4

Onna-musha Rising

The day after the funeral, Ashi summons two of her fellow onna-musha; Saitō, who is fully recovered by means of the tea; and another prominent young warrior to the western tainoya. They all arrive to find her standing behind a large rectangular table in the middle of the room. She appears different to them, more mature and serious-minded than they are used to seeing. Her disposition is not that of a young carefree girl any longer. Though the room itself is elaborate and beautifully arranged in a way to bring peace to their minds, her authoritative presence leads the guests to correctly surmise this is not a social call.

Around the long wooden table are four cushions, one for each of them. A simple and rustic meal of kuri gohan,[44] miso soup, and gozen-tachibana berries is accompanied by warm pots of tea. Behind Ashi is a six-paneled folding screen. The awe-inspiring screen depicts life near the tree of life in heaven and is meant to not only inspire them but remind them who they are and where they came from. Ashi invites Saitō to sit at the end of the table to her left. Miyo, widow

---

[44] Chestnuts and rice (translated from Japanese).

of Hatano Yoshimoto, takes her place across from Ashi and next to Saitō. Yui, Miyo's daughter and one of Ashi's closest friends, moves toward the next setting. Oishi Nakamura, Sasaki's son and a fine warrior in his own right, is invited to sit at the end of the table to Ashi's right. They all bow to her, and she returns it before taking her seat.

After sitting, Saitō politely surveys the table and, his appetite fully returned, says, "I am happy to receive so much food." Ashi is grateful he has healed; she offers him a polite smile. Without any conversation, they clean their hands with the provided towel and then begin eating. After all the food is gone and they have had their fill, Oishi says in gratitude, "It was quite a feast."

"Hai," answers Ashi, again with the polite smile of a gracious host. Her facial expression quickly turns serious though. "Please, make yourselves more comfortable if you wish. There is much to discuss. Specifically, we need to talk about betrayal and war." The whole mood of the chamber instantly becomes a little more tense. Ashi informs them of Ishida's betrayal and the Tsuchigumo clan. There has been much speculation over the last year as to what happened to him and the handful of men who vanished; now they all know the truth. She also tells them of the spider yōkai, Kumo; the locustlike monsters she plans to unleash; and Præsidiel, God's messenger. After they have all been brought up to speed, Ashi issues specific tasks. "Oishi-san is now samurai," she announces to all. Looking specifically at him, she directs, "You will recruit the ten best ashigaru for your squad."

"Hai," he says with a grateful bow.

"Yui, select the five best onna-musha. Give priority to those from the families of the fallen, so they may bring honor to those they have lost. Also, select the five best kyūdōka."[45]

---

[45] Archers (translated from Japanese).

"Hai."

"Miyo-san, you will reinforce our defenses and oversee the security of the Raikō estate. You must protect our people, during our absence."

"Hai, Ashi-sama."

"You have only today to select and prepare your troops. We depart tomorrow. Saitō will lead us to the tree where our warriors were ambushed. According to Præsidiel, the trail-head to the Shrine of Ancient Behemoths is near that tree. We will find it and make our way to the shrine. We must be prepared for all manner of yōkai and yūrei. Once we're there, Saitō and I will confront Ishida, Kumo, and her beast. Oishi, Yui, your ashigaru will cut down the Tsuchigumo and prevent any locust from escaping the abyss. These are not normal locusts either. Saitō was there when the one killed my father. He will instruct you and your warriors on how to fight them." The room is silent, each in their own contemplative thoughts. "Iku. Prepare for war."

"Hai!" they all exclaim. Everyone, save Saitō, leaves the room. There is no doubt among any of them that Ashi now commands the Hotaru-Raikō. They trust in her abilities as onna-musha and will readily follow her into battle.

"What do you wish of me while they go to gather their soldiers?" asks Saitō.

"Tell me everything you know of these beasts, and then spar with me for a while."

"Hai," he confirms, slightly grinning at the prospect of sparring with Ashi. "As you said, our adversary, the kaijū, has the appearance of a locust. His lengthy body is tan and speckled with black blotches. His long, and rather large, hind legs are lined with sharp spikes. Hidden under his wing shells is a scorpion's tail, which can curve up over his back. This is what killed Sasaki and your father." He pauses for a moment and looks down in mourning. "The monster's elongated head is almost human in appearance. He has great black oval eyes right in the front, instead of on each side like a normal locust. He has a mouth full of sharp fangs, resembling those of a large fox, and of tar-like spit. His black hair is that of a mad woman, disheveled and wild. And instead of two antennae, something like a golden crown curls up from his forehead and around his head."

"I see," replies Ashi as she stands. "Weak points?" she asks.

"None that I could see," he states as he too stands. "Like any locust, the underbelly between his front and middle legs?" Saitō ventures a guess.

Ashi leads them to a small dōjō behind the screen as they talk. "Our main enemy is Kumo, the one who summoned the kaijū. Unfortunately, I know no details of her other than hearsay from men of the Nara Prefecture."

In the dōjō, Ashi turns her back to Saitō; slips her arms out of her uchigi, exposing her white kosode underneath; and then ties the sleeves around her waist. She moves over to the weapons rack, picks up her shiai yo,[46] and turns to face Saitō. He takes a wooden bokken from the rack while grinning. Wasting no time, they bow. And Ashi immediately goes on the offensive, stabbing at him with her shiai yo. A bit later, Saitō disarms her, but she is quick to reach for a bokken from the rack and once again engage him. They frequently come to a stalemate in their practice, proving Ashi is highly skilled, exceptional really with both naginata and sword.

"Had enough, my lady?" asks Saitō brazenly.

Ashi smiles and, switching to hand-to-hand combat, lunges at her betrothed. They continue to spar until Ashi flips Saitō onto his back. She quickly straddles his stomach

---

[46] A practice naginata made of bamboo (translated from Japanese).

and raises the heel of her palm over his face signaling she can deliver the knockout blow. He looks up at her, smiles, and lets out a chuckle. Ashi reaches into her kosode and pulls out her fan. She smacks him on the forehead with it to remind him his inuendo is not appropriate but then leans down to whisper, "I love you."

"Will you still marry me if we return?" Saitō promptly asks.

"Hai."

"Yoi. Now let's take this outside so we can see how good you are in flight." Saitō flips her over his head, but he does not hear Ashi land on the ground. He jumps up and turns to see her hovering in the air. She smiles at him playfully, flies to grab her shiai yo, and then buzzes out of the house into the courtyard. "Hrmph," he grunts to himself. He strolls over, grabs his bokken, and takes flight after her. Out in the sunlight, they continue to spar for a little while.

Some children watch them training from the edges of the niwa. Ashi hears them giggling and thinks of her mother, who was always delighted in their presence. She does not let it distract her though. Near the end of their practice, Ashi and Saitō land close to each other in the courtyard. Although they are short of breath, they bow in respect to one another. They hear the little children cheer from near the base of the shrine. It makes them both smile.

*****

Later that night, Ashi has bathed and is dressed in a single white kosode with the orange uchigi her father gave her wrapped around her waist. Wisps of silken black hair dance in the evening breeze coming off the moat as she carries her naginata and her father's wakizashi up the path to the shrine.

It is her intent to pray not just for herself but also for the warriors who go with her in the morning.

Inside, she sets her weapons on the ground and quietly sits in the seiza position before the altar. Ashi reaches for her naginata first. She raises it over her head horizontally with both hands as she bows. Offering it to God, she gently places its long pole on the altar. She repeats her actions with her father's unsheathed sword. Once they have been presented, she bows low to pray. Unseen by her, her samurai, onna-musha, and ashigaru are beginning to gather around the base of the shrine. They are unable to explain why they come; they just feel drawn to it. They hear murmuring prayers in the dimly lit shrine above and join in. They bow their heads and offer their own petitions to God.

A strong, unexpected gust of wind blows through the shrine, extinguishing all the candles. Ashi stops her prayers and looks up. She hears the prayers of the warriors at the base of the shrine. The wind circles down the stone mount of the shrine and disperses into the gathered crowd. Everyone falls silent. Their attention lifts to the crisp night sky. Out of the starlit heavens, a bolt of lightning sizzles downward. Like water dropped on a stone, the lightning strikes the roof and splinters into several streams of blinding light. These streams curl out over the stone roof only to stream in through the openings of the shrine. They all meet again at the altar, striking the metal blades lying there. Sparks and embers explode into the air. The ground-shaking thunder that follows throws Ashi backward.

She quickly catches her breath, gets back on her feet, and collects herself. She is blinded by a pure white light. She holds her hand out in front of her face so it will cast a shadow over her eyes, allowing her to see what is happening. The brilliant light emanates from the bare blades of her father's sword and her own naginata. She falls on her knees before the altar.

Everyone on the ground below has witnessed this event. They see the pure white light emanating from all sides of the shrine. It illuminates the courtyard below and even the surrounding thicket. The glow quickly dims, and the night sky returns to normal. It takes a couple of minutes for their eyesight to readjust back to the night. Other villagers rush out of their homes, congregating at the southern side of the shrine mount to see what has taken place. These new onlookers point to the scabbards of the onna-musha and soldiers. A curious light seeps between their scabbards and sword guards. Some pull their swords slightly out exposing the white, glowing blades within. The Hotaru-Raikō know then that Kami has sent his blessing. In awe, they fall to their knees, bowing low from the seiza position.

Ashi hears the commotion below. She moves to the entrance and looks down at the crowd gathered there. Upon seeing her in the doorway, the people stand to greet her. A cheer erupts as Ashi emerges from the shrine. They know their onna-musha has risen. Ashi and her army are ready for tomorrow's journey.

*****

The heat of summer has passed. The mornings are cool, and the afternoons are pleasant. The Hotaru-Raikō prefer to travel in the warmer afternoon. A gentle southern breeze cools them as they stay close to the foothills along the northern side of the Kuzuryu River basin. It only takes a few hours of flight to reach the beech tree on the eastern side of the Takinami River. Ashi thinks it good strategy to arrive just before sunset. They will have enough daylight to locate the trailhead while using twilight, which is a time when the lines between reality and the mystical blur, to cloak their movements.

Saitō has led them to a towering beech tree growing up out of the side of a large hill. It grows at the tip of what looks like a mountainous peninsula surrounded by flat river basins. They approach cautiously but find no sign of the enemy or the bodies of their fallen warriors, both mysteries they are eager to solve. Feeling confident the tree is safe, Ashi flies to the top and rests in the canopy. Her army combs the area below for the hidden trailhead. Saitō stays with his beloved, keeping a watchful eye for the enemy; he has resolved to protect her better than he did her father.

Ashi has chosen to travel light, wearing only her orange chest plate, shoulder armor, and forearm guards over a single gray kosode and her favorite orange and white hakama. Her father's wakizashi is tucked securely in her obi, while her naginata rests across her legs. Most of her jet-black hair is collected into a ponytail resting on her back; she leaves her beauty strands free to sway in the treetop breeze. She takes a deep breath and exhales slowly. It is a short but pleasant respite; and, although she faces a great unknown, she is calm.

From their vantage point, the whole base of Hakusan is laid out before them. At first, Ashi's focus is on the mountain itself. The setting sun is warm on her back as she meditates on the beauty of the mountain's trinitarian peaks. Soon, her line of sight begins to move downward though, until it comes upon a wooded ravine that seems to snake through the middle of the foothill peninsula below. Not far off to the east, she spies large spiderwebs holding back broken branches in the underbrush at the edge of a small field. She points at it and asks, "Saitō, there, in the ravine? The webs holding back those branches, do they resemble the webs you found near the hot springs?"

"Hai." He motions for two ashigaru to join him. "I will investigate and return."

She watches her samurai fly down, hand on his sword handle and ready for combat. He slows as he approaches the opening. The two soldiers fan out to his left and right. After they conduct a brief reconnaissance from the air, they return. Saitō reports, "There is a faded animal trail there. It does not appear to be well marked or often traveled. I believe this is the trailhead we seek."

"Yoi. Let's wait here just a bit longer. It's not quite time to enter yet," she patiently instructs. The sun is sinking lower in the sky.

It isn't long before hues of pinks and oranges fill the heavens, while evening shadows creep across the land. A faint mist begins to form in the river basins around them. Ashi knows it will soon blanket the trail and obscure the old forest. "Omagatoki," she mumbles. "The end of the day when the yōkai emerge." She takes a deep breath. "Saitō-san, rally everyone to me." Her mood has changed, and her tone reflects the strength of her father. "Prepare them to enter the trail."

"Hai, Ashi-sama."

CHAPTER 5

Revelations of the Yōkai

The Hotaru-Raikō assemble in the treetop awaiting their commander's orders. Ashi stands in the bough of the highest branch, watching and waiting for the fog to move up the slope of the foothills. She knows it will conceal their incursion. As soon as it nears the field, she grasps her naginata in both hands and, without hesitation, flies down into the open trailhead. Her militia follows swiftly and silently. Wisps of mist swirl in the air with the beats of their wings as they pierce the webbed opening, one after another, like threading a needle.

They discover the road to the shrine has been overgrown. Unused by man, it has been reduced to the size of an animal trail. There are many tracks following the now winding path; some are clearly from the Tsuchigumo clan, but others are unknown. Yui directs her kyūdōka into the trees on each side of the path. They fly from branch to branch, forming a perimeter around those walking the trail. Their thigh armor glows white, allowing the rest to always know where they are. As they move from tree to tree, occasionally flashing their lights, they appear as normal hotaru so as to not draw unwanted attention. Everyone else is on foot, led by Ashi and Saitō.

The fog blankets the thick forest underbrush, making the trail difficult to follow. It dissipates the farther inward they travel; however, the landscape becomes darker and unnaturally silent. Then, about a kilometer down the trail, subtle *Whoosh* sounds are heard all around them in the spaces between the trail and the archers. Onibi burst into existence there. These blue, flamelike spirits are always thought to be malevolent, so Ashi gives the signal to stop. Everyone is still as the onibi fly about, just above the underbrush. They appear to be taunting and tempting some of the soldiers and onna-musha to come closer. Ashi watches them carefully before finally commanding, "Move forward, but stay on the trail. Keep your distance from them; do not disturb the onibi."

As they begin walking, one orb of light comes dangerously close to the trail near Yui. It manifests a face, one that she instantly recognizes. "Papa?" she asks as she unconsciously raises her hand to touch the flaming orb.

Ashi hears her. She turns to see Yui raising her hand and reaching for the orb. "Īe!" she exclaims. "Don't touch it."

Yui is shocked out of her trance. She lowers her hand, saying somewhat shamefully, "Sumimasen,[47] Ashi-sama."

As soon as she says it, taiko drums begin beating. They all recognize them as the same ones heard days ago. This time, however, they are loud and close. The onibi begin to vibrate and flicker. It's almost as if they were fighting against something. What they resist becomes all too apparent when they are suddenly pulled by an unknown force down the trail and almost out of sight. "We must move, now! Follow the onibi," orders Ashi. She runs as quickly and quietly as her

---

[47] I'm sorry (translated from Japanese).

waraji sandals will carry her. They follow the streaking flames until they come to an abrupt halt another kilometer down the trail. Ashi again gives the signal to stop.

The rhythm of the drums is slow and steady. Ashi watches one of the onibi get sucked into a squat stone ishidōrō hidden among the tall grass and old trees. Looking down the trail, she realizes the other flaming spirits are being pulled into other stone lanterns, which mark the right side of the old shrine road. The eerie lights follow the twisting and turning path into the distance. The drums boom louder, and their pace begins to quicken. The mist starts to thin out, pulling back into the woods.

Saitō moves up to examine the first light. The retreating fog's wispy edges lick at the ancient, moss-covered lantern. Inside the onibi has taken the form of a man, who thrashes about seeking to escape his new prison. The spirit, now aware he is being observed, calms down, affording him a closer look. Saitō gasps. "It is Yoshimoto-san, Yui's father. These ishidōrō…they're prisons," he says, looking back at Ashi. She runs up to observe for herself. "The onibi we encountered must be the trapped spirits of those Hotaru-Raikō who were cut down recently. Who could have done this?" he asks.

"Kumo," replies Ashi. "If she can summon the kaijū, she can be the only one capable of this wicked spell. We must bring an end to this." She stands and motions for the rest to follow. They resume traveling the now faintly lit trail. Light from the nearly full white moon pierces the twisted canopy of leafless trees overhead. Its light casts shadows among the swaying grasses and flickering ishidōrō. The tempo of the drums quickens as they advance. Ashi feels her heart throb in time with the drums; it synchronizes with the sound of their steps.

Always watching her kyūdōka in the trees, she notices they have stopped at the crest of a small hill. She calls her ashigaru to a halt before going up the hill to see why they have stopped. There are only two more lanterns in the distance. A giant figure moves in the shadows past the last ishidōrō. She ducks in the foliage on the right side of the road, a few feet behind the lantern at the top of the hill. Saitō moves up and takes cover in the shadows on the left side of the trail. They wait for the figure to come into the light.

The tempo of the drums subsides a little. Something draws Ashi's eye to the ishidōrō. The figure inside is that of a woman sitting still with her head down. She sneaks closer for a better look. At first the spirit barely moves. Ashi moves closer, peering into the lantern. The spirit reluctantly raises her head to look at her visitor. It is her mother, Harumi.

Ashi gasps and slides back to her hiding place. Saitō sneaks across the road to her. "What is it?" he asks.

"In the lantern…" She is clearly saddened. "It is my mother. Her spirit is trapped within the stone prison." She stands back up and slowly approaches the ishidōrō. Saitō follows her. He can see the water collecting in the corners of her dark eyes. She peers through the flickering flame into the eyes of her mother. "Okaa-san,"[48] she whispers. Harumi's spirit cannot speak; she only looks upon her daughter with love. Ashi reaches toward her mother, who immediately signals her to stop. Remembering her own advice to Yui, she quickly withdraws her hand.

Saitō witnesses a change in her expression. Anger swells in Ashi for the evil done to her mother and her people. She resolves to bring this curse to an end. She shifts her body to stare down toward the cave and mutters to herself, "Kumo."

---

[48] Mother (translated from Japanese).

69

From this vantage point, she watches the figure moving in the distance.

A torii made from the cracked bleached-white bones of prehistoric creatures stands in stark contrast to the darkness of the cave, which it sits in front of. Between the torii and the last ishidōrō, branches that look like twisted, boney hands reach out over the trail from each side. The roots of tall, slender trees with no foliage snake through the coarse dark rocks where the old road ends. She notices human skulls and other bones intertwined with the roots near the base of their trunks. The trees look almost as if they, too, were guarding the entrance. Ashi stares intently at the dark sap-like substance that glistens as it oozes down the bark in the faint moonlight. Suddenly it dawns on her what she is seeing: jubokko trees. She has heard tale of these vampiric plants. They do not drink water, only blood. These trees look parched too. Clearly, they are positioned in this valley of death to capture curious visitors.

Just then, a tengu, the size of a human, walks out of the cave, through the torii, and into the light. The drums beat quietly enough so the talons on his black, birdlike feet can be heard clicking on the stone as he walks. He stops to inspect the wilderness, making sure those inside the shrine are not disturbed. Although details of his features are difficult to see in the low light, his red face and long, beak-like nose stand out against his white windblown hair and pointy beard. He holds his dingy, tattered, and unpreened gray wings upward as though he were about to take flight. He wears maroon armor over a black kosode, with maroon hakama tucked into ebony shin guards. The only other armor he wears are maroon forearm guards. In his right hand is a spear and in his left a lantern.

The kyūdōka have observed all they can and begin to fly horizontally back down the hill toward the rest of the clan. They flash their lights regularly every few seconds, mirroring the beat of the drums. The tengu spots them and watches. Soon, with a voice that sounds like the cawing of a crow, he grumbles, "*Baah!* Just firefly in the woods." He holds up a faded, old chochin-obake,[49] looking to see if there is anything else out in the forest. Two weary eyes peer out from between the ghostly lantern's old ribs near its top. Near the bottom, its internal wooden ribs have split, giving it the appearance of a gaping mouth. Thin black strands of hair hang around the face on the lantern, which resembles an old, wrinkly woman. A spectral light shines out of its yawning mouth, eerily illuminating the old road past the two jubokko.

Seeing nothing else of concern, he plants the bottom of his spear on the stone. The tengu sets the ghostly lantern on the ground, which lets out a hissing groan of disappointment. "Stop your moaning, obake!" he caws. He then stands at rest directly in front of the gate listening to drums. Their tempo is picking back up.

Ashi knows the time to strike is now, but before she can give orders to her warriors, the flame of her mother's spirit crackles. Ashi moves back behind the lantern to look at her. Harumi's spirit motions with her hands to give her something. Ashi thinks for a second and then waves for Yui, who immediately runs up. "Give me an arrow," she whispers. Yui complies and hands her an arrow from her quiver. Ashi gently places the tip of the arrow into the ishidōrō. "Please, Mother, grant us use of your flame." Harumi smiles softly at the wisdom of her daughter; she knows their hearts and minds are still connected. She places her hands upon the arrow tip. The blue flame of the onibi envelopes the arrowhead. Ashi bows

---

49 Paper lantern ghost (translated from Japanese).

her head reverently. "Arigatou, Okaa-san." She lifts her eyes. "I will end this curse, Mother."

She turns to hand the arrow back to Yui and instructs, "Gather your kyūdōka. Spread the flame to one arrow for each of them. Two of your archers will aim for the jubokko, and three will aim for the tengu's wings. Saitō and I will fly in to kill the tengu as he burns. Everyone else will ensure any unseen enemies in and around the cave are cut down. Iku."

"Hai, Ashi-sama!"

Ashi waits for Yui to pass the flame to the kyūdōka, who have rejoined the rest behind the crest of the hill. She then watches them fan out along the ridge and prepare for attack. Kneeling in the underbrush, the archers quietly slide their arms out of the left side of their kosode, exposing their bare arms and chests; the women archers wear muneate, or leather breast plates. This will ensure nothing will interfere with the flight of their arrows. Slowly knocking a flame-tipped arrow, they rise in unison, stealthily draw their bowstrings, and take aim. Ashi, Saitō, and the rest have gathered on the trail and are ready. The taiko drums are reaching a crescendo.

*****

Deep inside the cave, the flickering torchlit shrine, deep gray and black basalt columns rise straight up, curving at the top toward a central vault. Natural light does not reach this far back into the cavern. The Tsuchigumo have mounted long, rust-plagued iron torches to every fourth column, which reach out into the unholy cathedral from both sides. The fallen Hotaru-Raikō, wrists tied together, hang over the torches by their bound hands. They have been stripped of their armor, their heads hang low, and their lifeless eyes look down upon the black volcanic gravel beneath their bare feet. Strange, vile markings have been carved into their bare chests. The stench of death blankets the cavernous shrine.

The cathedral-like cavern itself becomes more and more narrow as the basalt columns lead toward a huge doorway in the back. Framed by an arch made of rib bones from prehistoric creatures, two slabs of dark-gray andesite with flecks of white crystal seal the long-hidden entrance to the abyss. Kumo stands before the stone doors with her hands raised. All eight of her hairy, black spider legs extend outward from her back too. Her servant Ishida stands behind and to her left. The locust kaijū paces back and forth between them and the drums.

In the middle of the cave is a small stage, upon which sits an odaiko (big drum). Each side has a drumhead, the diameter of which is about one foot across. That means each drumhead is slightly longer than the height of the average Hotaru-Raikō. Tanned hides stretch across each head in stark contrast to the ebony wood of the drum itself. It is mounted on a rack also made from the bones of the ancient behemoths. Two of Ishida's soldiers drum a side of the odaiko, producing a low, loud, and deep rhythm. Closer to the entrance, and on either corner of the stage behind the big drum, are two smaller daiko. They carry a faster, higher-pitch sound. The soldiers shout occasionally with intensity as they bang on these drums; they know they are close to breaking the seal on the doors and pour everything they've got into their performance.

*****

Ashi gives the signal. The kyūdōka let loose their volley. Streaks of blue flame sizzle down the small hill through the night sky, each one striking its intended target. The blood-starved and dry jubokko are quickly engulfed in scorching flame, their branches creaking and cracking as they flail about in pain. The arrows striking the tengu's wings quickly ignite his unkept feathers, and fire spreads. He drops his spear and desperately flaps his wings while attempting to pat out the spreading fire with his hands. Ashi grips her naginata, and Saitō draws his sword. They take flight, giving a fearsome war cry as they drive forward between the crackling flames of the burning jubokko.

*****

Inside, a sudden loud crack echoes through the shrine. Eon-old dust shakes loose from the seals around the doors. The drums have worked; they have broken the seal. Ishida raises his hand in the air. Clinching a fist, he signals the drummers to stop.

*****

The drums stop, and the tengu hears the war cries of the Hotaru-Raikō. It is too late for him though as he realizes they are upon him. Ashi and Saitō plunge their white-bladed weapons deep into his chest, piercing his heart. The tengu lets out a loud but diminishing caw as he perishes. He falls to the ground with a thud, crushing the chochin-obake beneath his burning corpse. Ashi hears a rush of movement inside the cave; she knows the enemy has been alerted to their presence.

*****

Just after the last reverberating drumbeat dissipates, the death cry of the tengu comes echoing in. Surprised, Ishida looks over his shoulder. The kaijū wheels around to face the shrine entrance. The black spittle from his putrid mouth splatters on the odaiko drum. Ishida steps forward to Kumo and says, "We have been discovered."

Kumo reaches to caress his face with the back of her hand and says in a sweet, seductive voice, "It matters not, lover. They come to their doom."

"Hai!" exclaims Ishida. He removes the devil's mask from his belt, slides it over his distorted face, and turns toward the entrance. Kumo motions to the two odaiko drummers to attend to the doors. Ishida signals for the rest of his retainers to move out against the unknown enemy. The locust creature lets out a deep guttural laugh as he too eagerly awaits a battle.

*****

Saitō signals to the kyūdōka and other warriors to create a semicircle around the cave entrance, while the rest of the force moves down the trail. He joins Ashi in the middle of the old road in front of the cave. "They will be coming soon," he informs softly.

"Let them come," answers Ashi. There is a ferocity in her eyes he has never seen before. She hovers in midair with her naginata in both hands, poised for the coming fight. Her graceful figure is silhouetted against the blue light of the flames consuming the vampiric trees at her back.

75

It isn't long before a small force of Tsuchigumo comes rushing toward Ashi and her Hotaru-Raikō. Their hearts, filled with a murderous rage, fuel the wicked red lights of their armor and weapons as they streak through the blackness of the cave. In their blind rage, they fly straight for Saitō and Ashi. The kyūdōka lose a volley of white-tipped arrows striking four of the five enemy soldiers. The fifth warrior, who is in the middle, rapidly rises into the air and then plunges downward toward them with sword drawn. Fast as lightning, Ashi streaks upward to meet him in the air. The enemy gives a loud war cry as he gets close. Ashi swiftly turns her body and, with a fluid upward slice of her naginata, cleanly severs the head of the attacking traitor. She comes to an upright position, hovering high above the cave entrance as the enemy's body falls to the ground. The initial battle, which is swift and short-lived, energizes the Raikō clan. They give a unified cheer of victory.

*****

The yōkai and her henchmen hear the cheer as it echoes inward. They know it is not their own who cheer. Suddenly panicked, Kumo asks Ishida, "Who moves against us?"

"I'm not certain. We have eliminated the strongest warriors of the Hotaru-Raikō. Only their onna-musha are left, and they are too weak, too unskilled."

"Whoever it is, they will be no match for the devil's army. Hold them off until we can open the doors." Kumo's tone has changed; she is alarmed. She turns to shout at the remaining two clansmen, "Pull, you idiots!"

There is a faint yellow-orange sliver of light shining through from between the doors and around its edges. Above the doors, a foul-smelling smoke seeps upward into the vaulted ceiling.

*****

Ashi leaves the archers at the entrance to the cave to protect the invading force and to prevent anyone, or anything, from escaping. She and Saitō lead the remainder into the cave. Keeping the distant, yellow-orange light in their sights, they fly cautiously into the cavern. The light grows brighter as they approach. Odd sounds echo off the cave walls. Ashi realizes Kumo has succeeded in breaking the seal on the gate and their time is running out. They emerge into the underground chamber, lighting on the ground just behind the drums, and quickly take in the horrible scene.

Appalled, Ashi gasps upon seeing the long-dead bodies of her people hang lifeless from the walls. Kumo stands between the drums and the opening door. She keeps her back to the invading Hotaru-Raikō; her spindly legs stretched out to make her easily identifiable. Ashi assumes the warrior to the left of Kumo in the devil's mask can only be Ishida, the traitor. He has clearly embraced the darkness she saw within him. Taking up the right half of the room, the locust-like monster looms large. He rattles his wing covers over his back in anticipation of battle. The tar-like spit Saitō previously described drips from his open maw. Two Tsuchigumo tug at the doors at the back of the shrine.

The stone gate lurches open a bit more. A foul, stale fog churns through the cracks like the smoke from the swordsmith's furnace. It boils upward, filling the cavern vault and obscuring everyone's sight. The smog smells of death and decay. Clattering of insect wings echoes in the void beyond. Ashi can sense the contempt and the rage coming from an unseen foe. She hears gnashing of teeth and the dripping of black spittle on smoldering stones.

"Hear that?" the beast gurgles, his gaze fixed upon Ashi. "My brothers yearn to be free." A grim smile spreads across his hideous face. "They yearn to taste your flesh. Heh-heh-heh." He does his best to disturb her, to make her uneasy, but she says nothing in response.

Saitō settles his gaze upon Ishida. He wants to restore his honor and avenge the daimyō's death. "Traitor," he blurts out. Ishida laughs in contempt, opens his wing covers, spreads his wings, and then slowly rises into the smoke collecting in the vault above. He draws his sword, its bloodred light slowly growing brighter in the thick, black haze. Saitō, his blazing white sword already in hand, lets out a loud battle cry and flies swiftly upward to engage him in combat. Their swords clang loudly; bright sparks briefly illuminate the two samurai in the hellish fog. The smoke thickens so that only the light of their swords is seen.

"Yui. Oishi. Close those doors!" commands Ashi. They immediately take flight, leading the rest of the army around the right side of the beast. With a surprisingly fast and mighty thrust, the kaijū pins one of the soldiers against the basalt wall with his rear leg. Ashi knows he is off-balance and lunges toward his left and Kumo. Rapidly closing in on her target, she swings her naginata down from the right side to put an end to the villainess. The locust chooses to release the warrior, giving him just enough time to whip his tail around and stop her killing blow. He does not, however, stop her blade from slicing through one of Kumo's spindly black legs. Kumo screams as she pulls the rest of her legs in toward her back.

Yui and Oishi rush to the doors. One of the Tsuchigumo soldiers turns, draws his sword, and, in a downward arc, cuts through Oishi's armor and into his left forearm. Oishi, filled with adrenaline, counters, running his sword through the enemy's chest with just his right hand. Yui pushes past Oishi and, her naginata having a length advantage, strikes down the other soldier before he can draw his weapon. She looks back at Oishi with concern, but he leaves his sword in the enemy and rushes to the right door. Hitting it with his right shoulder, he grunts as he attempts to push it. Yui follows suit and leans onto the left door, pushing as hard as she can. They hear a clatter rising from the abyss, like armored horses charging. A force hits the doors on the other side. The other locusts are trying to break free. The rest of the ashigaru surge to help close the doors too. It is a stalemate.

In the smokey haze above, white and red blades continue to clash. Rising, falling, slashing, and clanging, the swords move about furiously in the air, wielded by unseen warriors.

The red blade makes a downward strike. The white blade, moving upward, deflects it, whirls with hurricane force in the air, and finds its target. The movement of the red blade stops. It hangs tip down in the air for a few seconds before falling to the ground with a clanging sound. Ishida's headless body lands next to it with a thud. The head lands nearby; lifeless black eyes peer out from behind the red devil's mask. Saitō has avenged his daimyō.

Ashi, still holding down on the beast's scorpion tail, watches helplessly as Kumo casts a web upward and pulls herself to the cave vault above. The smoke hides her from everyone's view. She sees Saitō's blade in the ashen fog nearby. "Saitō!" screams Ashi. "Kumo is escaping." Just then he is brushed aside by something scurrying past him. Swirls of dense smoke waft past him. He swings his blade blindly but strikes nothing.

Below, Ashi can feel the locust's tail slide down the pole of her naginata. She knows she is no match for his strength, but she is highly confident in her own speed. She spins to her left, releasing his tail. As she spins, she turns her naginata down and then back up, driving the luminous blade through the exoskeleton of the venom bulb. He screams and whips his tail backward, yanking the naginata from her hands. He staggers toward the right wall, lifting the front of his body up. Ashi, seeing the opportunity, rapidly draws her father's wakizashi and slashes downward through his chest armor. As she does, Saitō zooms downward, grasps the handle of her naginata, and drives the tip into the seam between two basalt columns. The kaijū is trapped.

Ashi stands before him with the tip of her father's sword pressed against the locust's throat. Saitō stands to her left, ready to strike if necessary. The locust looks at them both and laughs. "My brothers are only permitted to torment humans.

But you, little pests, you we can kill. What pleasure your deaths will bring." He coughs up a vile black saliva. "Even if you stop us today, we will be released again and…"—he coughs again—"when we are will seek your kind out first. We will erase you from the land. We—" Without a word, Ashi swiftly separates his head from his body. The killing stroke is so swift that tiny arcs of lightning reach out from her sword into the air around her and some connecting with the stone wall. As his long head hits the ground, his golden crown makes a *tink, tink, tink* sound as it rolls on the gravel and stone underfoot.

Ashi wipes the foul-smelling blood from her father's sword and returns it to its sheath. She turns her attention first to the doors and then glances at her beloved Saitō. "Quickly, find Kumo," she commands.

"Hai," he answers before rushing toward the shrine entrance.

Ashi walks toward the doors. A calmness overtakes her. Her father's voice echoes in her mind, *Our Lord once taught, "If you have faith even the size of a mustard seed, you can say to this mountain, 'Move from here to there,' and it will move. Nothing will be impossible for you." You are destined to do great things, daughter. Keep your faith in God. And you, too, will be able to move mountains.* It was one of the many lessons she learned when he walked with her as a youth, comforting and instructing her.

Now Ashi walks fearlessly toward the crack between the doors. The firelight piercing the doors flashes across her dark eyes. Yui, a wounded Oishi, and the rest of her ashigaru strain to close the gate. She stops a few feet in front of them. Sitting in the seiza position, she closes her eyes and places her palms together in front of her in prayer. Her warriors look at her curiously. The black fog is starting to settle to the ground too, while the beastly locusts rage and clatter on the other side of the doors. She begins her prayer, "Kami, my father taught me that with even a small amount of faith in you, I could move mountains. I may not understand your ways, Lord, but I believe in you. I know the time has not come for these wretched creatures to be released upon the world. So I place my trust in you that you will help us this night. Let these doors be closed and sealed once more according to your will." A stillness falls upon the room. There is silence. Then, the massive andesite slabs begin grinding slowly against the volcanic gravel floor. The doors start to slowly close.

*****

Outside, the kyūdōka watch the cave entrance. Bows at the ready, they watch and listen intently, trying to discern what is happening. Thick black smoke bellows out of the cave. It hugs the roof of the entrance before dissipating into the night sky. The faithful archers hear something approaching rapidly. It stops before emerging. They train their lightning-tipped arrows at the entrance. Then, coming out slowly, holding Kumo's black and crimson jūnihitoe, is Saitō. The kyūdōka lower their arrows.

"Where is the yōkai, Kumo?" he calls. "Did she come out?"

"Īe," responds the lead archer.

"Kuso!" he curses. He turns and, looking up, sees the smoke bellowing out of the entrance. He walks back to the mouth of the cave. On the ground, shimmering in the low light, he finds a small pool of blood just below the roof of the cave opening. He kneels to inspect it and notices a light trail of blood leading back into the shrine from the pool. A single drop falls from the roof into the pool. *Hrmm...* He thinks.

She must have returned to spider form, used the dark color of her body to blend in with the smoke, and then escaped unseen. He motions to the archers to follow him back into the Shrine of Ancient Behemoths.

*****

Saitō and the rest arrive back inside just in time to witness the doors close with a thunderous boom. He sees Ashi on the ground in front of the doors and, thinking she might be injured, runs to her. As soon as he is beside her, he realizes she is praying. Lightning suddenly flashes along with each door seal, startling the Hotaru-Raikō. God has sealed the doors. She places her hands in the gravel and gives a low bow, saying softly, "Thank you, Kami." She gracefully rises to her feet afterward and smiles at all her exhausted warriors. A few were injured, but not one has lost their life in the battle. Though the highest goal for a samurai is to die in the service of the Lord, too many have already fallen; she is grateful none had to make that sacrifice this night.

Most of the ashigaru had witnessed her strength, her skill with the naginata. A few saw her faith. All respect her authority as their leader. She looks around at her faithful retainers, each bowing as she looks in their direction, even her betrothed when she turns to him. "Saitō-san," she asks, "Kumo?"

"Vanished in the night. She fled under the cover of that terrible smoke."

Ashi, ever so slightly, purses her lips and lowers her head, disappointed she escaped. She takes a breath and exhales. Raising her head up, she looks into his eyes. With a loving firmness, she directs, "Take charge. Lead the others. Take our honored dead down from the walls and bring them outside. Make the proper funeral pyres so we can collect their bones for burial later. Gather the traitors and the beast. Pile them up in front of the doors. They are cursed and must remain here. Drag the torii down, destroy the drums, and cut down what remains of the jubokko. Bring all remnants of this accursed shrine into the cave. When done, we will raze it to the ground. The Shrine of the Ancient Behemoths is to be no more."

"Hai, Ashi-sama." He immediately sets everyone to task.

Ashi walks to the doors where Yui and Oishi are. She has noticed their lights are brighter when they are together. She calls to them, "Yui-san. Oishi-san." They bow again in respect. After they stand, she motions to see Oishi's arm. He raises it and turns it so she can inspect his wound. "Yui, take Oishi outside. Clean and dress his wound." She pauses for a second to offer them a smile. "Afterward, help the others light the pyres." They bow and then rush out into the night air together.

Ashi strides over to the locust. She yanks her naginata from his scorpion tail. Lifeless, it falls to the ground. She turns and glides just above the gravelly floor toward the entrance. Outside, her eyes follow the last of the putrid smoke as it trickles up through the trees. The dark sky is filled with stars. Unable to ignore their beauty, she stares at them for a moment. Turning her sight back down to the old road, she notices all the old ishidōrō are empty; the onibi are gone. *Mama?* she wonders. *Have their spirits been set free?*

The Hotaru-Raikō spend the rest of the night gently removing their own honored dead, tearing down the shrine, and depositing the cursed remains near the stone doors. After everyone has completely evacuated the cave, Ashi lights a torch from one of the funeral pyres. She then flies into the wicked domain and sets the ruins ablaze.

Saitō later watches his beloved emerge with a deep fascination. Her beauty strands sway as she flies out slowly. Though soot- and bloodstained, her bright orange and white jūnihitoe ripples and flows about her. Her womanly figure, again silhouetted by fire, is carried elegantly by her delicate wings. It is as though she entered a cocoon of a cave and emerged a woman. A shiver runs down his spine as he experiences a soul-deep attraction to her. She lands gracefully at his side and turns to watch the shrine burn. He sees only her though; he wants nothing more than to be with her for the rest of his life.

The yellow-orange glow emanating from deep within the blackened cave is eerie. The whole clan stands in the chilly predawn air staring into what looks like the eye of an ancient, malevolent goliath looking back at them. The forest is still and silent, but not for long. Ashi orders them to break the stones and fill in the opening of the cavern. Everyone happily complies, sealing off the accursed gate to the abyss. They leave the area unmarked, praying the forest will overgrow and further hide the vile place.

*****

Dirty, tired, and a little banged up, the Hotaru-Raikō have followed the faded animal trail back out of the woods. Serenity descends upon them as they move out into the open field where they began their mission. The familiar early morning glow is on the eastern horizon, and birdsong has returned to the woods. A wet dew has settled upon the long grass in the field. Ashi decides to rest there before going back to their home on the banks of the Fukui Castle moat.

She flies up to rest on a large branch of the same beech tree she perched in the day before. Her onna-musha, samurai, and ashigaru sip dew from the grasses and wash their faces. Looking around for Saitō, who is strangely not to be found anywhere, she catches a glimpse of Yui also resting alone in the long grass. She wonders where Oishi has gone off to as well. A slight breeze causes the tree to sway. The gentle wind also takes her back to her childhood, to a time when she sat with her father in such a tree. She recalls her father's words, "I love the beech tree. Its shape reminds me of the tree of life." This whole trial has opened her eyes to her father's positivity. No matter what danger he faced, no matter what tasking or how firm he had to be with her or his soldiers, he always saw the good in others, in nature, and in God. She reflects on how positive he was, in almost every situation. She smiles to herself, whispering, "Hai, Papa, it is going to be a good day."

Just then Saitō zooms up and over the treetop. She is so deep in thought that he startles her a bit. His breath is labored as he lands, but he is smiling from ear to ear. In his hands are two plump, bright-red, gozen-tachibana berries. "I thought you would be hungry," he says, offering her one.

"What about the others?" she asks selflessly.

"Ha!" He laughs. "You are your father's daughter, always thinking about others. Look." He nods his head for her to look down. Oishi takes a berry from a makeshift bag, made from a large leaf, and then hands the bag to one of the other warriors to pass around. The berry he took he offers to Yui. "Oishi and I thought it would be good to bring you, and the others, some well-earned food." He presents the berry to Ashi again. She smiles at him and accepts the fruit. He sits down next to her and exhales. There is no doubt about the love they share for one another.

She and Saitō politely eat their berries and watch the yellow-orange light of the sun crest slowly over Hakusan. Once again, its glorious beams of light reach out toward the sky in many directions. Some of the rays stretch down across the land, chasing the shadows away. The warmth of the light kisses Ashi's fair skin and warms her supple cheeks; she is rejuvenated by it.

They linger for a while before she flies down to the rest, announcing, "It is a new dawn. God has blessed us. Let us return to our families and our homes." Her warriors, rested and fed, give her a rousing cheer. Ashi takes them to the sky and leads them all home.

EPILOGUE

Soaring Spirits

Many miles away, on the western side of Mount Fuji, a darkness settles in the Aokigahara Forest. A deposed kōgō, a seven-legged spider, haunts the once pristine forest. Harboring a profound hatred for man and hotaru alike, the yōkai named Kumo sometimes takes the form of a small woman in the trees, a beautiful fairy to man's eyes. She whispers to lost and weary travelers as they walk, tempting them to despair. She convinces weak-minded men to see no value in their lives and knows when they have fallen into her trap. For these hopeless lost, she spins the webbing for a noose and offers it as a gift, an invitation to be free of their sorrow. Many have succumbed to her wicked and troubling murmurs, hanging themselves from the very branches upon which she sits. Now Kumo is never alone; she captures and keeps these yūrei, the spirits of the hanged, for herself. To this day she feeds on their eternal souls, extending her own unnatural life.

*****

In the secluded Raikō Village, a full week has passed since the destruction of the forsaken shrine. A beautiful onna-musha and a dashing samurai have made the lengthy procession up the rock pathway into the Shrine of Watashi. There the young couple proclaim their vows before God and then lovingly exchange cups filled with nectar with each other. They soon emerge from the old ishidōrō as husband and wife to a rousing cheer. Descending into the niwa, Ashi and Saitō are celebrated by their clan, their kin, and their firefly cousins as lord and lady of the Hotaru-Raikō.

After their congratulatory welcome, they return to their shinden to change into less formal attire. They hear the reception gather outside in the courtyard. It is a rare occasion for extravagance. Music, singing, dancing, firefly light displays, and, of course, Sumai no Sechi elevate the spirits of the entire village.

During a Sumai no Sechi match, which, like her father before her, Saitō is completely engrossed in, an odd feeling comes over Ashi. She begins to look around, searching the festivities taking place around her. Her gaze is pulled toward the ishidōrō shrine. There, leaning against the wall next to the door is a quiet visitor. Her dark almond eyes meet the light-blue eyes of Præsidiel. He stands upright and, with a pleasing smile, nods to her. She humbly bows her head in return. In her heart, she feels the affirmation and love of God. Having given his smile of praise and approval, Præsidiel spreads his wings and takes flight into the heavens above. Ashi happily returns her attention to her husband and the courtyard games.

*****

Later in the evening, after the feasting and festivities have ended, Ashi walks with Saitō along the eastern rō leading out to the open-air pavilion. Though she is generally happy, it is clear something still weighs heavily upon her mind. She hides her sadness behind the fan in her hand. In truth, she misses her parents. She desperately wishes she knew what happened to her mother's spirit. She also still desires her father's blessing on their marriage. They walk the entire length of the rō in silence, Saitō patiently waiting for her to open up to him.

Upon reaching the pavilion, Ashi strolls out into the middle and stares up. Something moves in the star-laden sky. Barely noticeable by Ashi at first, two bright white stars rise, fall, and encircle each other. She unknowingly lowers her fan. Saitō looks up, too, trying to see what has captured her attention. He, too, sees the dancing lights.

Not knowing what she is witnessing, she watches the lights intently as they descend. There seems to be a familiar rhythm in their movement as if she had seen it before. *Wait,* she thinks to herself. *I recognize that dance.* Her heart leaps with joy. *That is the way Otousan danced with Okaa-san. Could it be?*

The flickering lights draw much closer. They twirl and swoop to just a few feet over the newlyweds. Ashi looks at Saitō with a joyous smile on her face. He is still staring at the puzzling lights. He looks down at his bride. She beams with an infectious smile and twinkling eyes. He has seen that look enough to know she is about to do something, but what? She opens her wing covers and spreads her wings. "Ah," he mutters, "you're going to dance with the lights." Saitō quickly extends his wings, too, as Ashi is already lifting off the ground. He reaches up to take her hand.

They rise together into the night sky. The starlike lights spin around them both. Ashi giggles and laughs cheerfully as if she were a child. Saitō is caught up in her delight. A feeling of pure joy and wonder fills their hearts as the dancing goes on for a brief time. Soon it ends though, and the twinkling lights hover right in front of them both. Ashi hears her father's voice, "Well done, daughter... Well done." Tears of joy well up in her dark almond-shaped eyes.

They know the time has come for her father and mother to ascend. She and Saitō humbly bow. As the spirits ascend, Ashi leans onto Saitō's chest. He wraps his arm around her lower back, under her wings. Together they watch the two lights soar rapidly into the sky until they are indistinguishable from the rest of the flickering stars in the deep purple sky.

So begins an enduring peace for the Hotaru-Raikō.

The End

ABOUT THE AUTHOR

John Eudy is a twenty-six-year military veteran. He was both a soldier in the Army National Guard and a sailor in the US Coast Guard. Having lived in ten different towns and cities in five states and having visited forty other states and territories, including Guam, he is well traveled. He retired from military service in 2015.

After spending three short years working in the civilian sector, John officially retired to pursue his dream of becoming a published author. Inspired by faith and scripture, he enjoys weaving history, cultural legends, life experiences, and Christian morality into fictional tales.

John and his family currently reside in their native Missouri. He has been married to his lovely wife of over twenty-five years, and they are the proud parents of four daughters, two of which are already with God in heaven.

CPSIA information can be obtained
at www.ICGtesting.com
Printed in the USA
JSHW011909120722
28039JS00004B/47

9 781685 707606